D1106487

MYSTERIOUS, MENACING & MACABRE

EDITED BY HELEN HOKE

A Chilling Collection
Demons Within
Eerie, Weird and Wicked
Ghostly, Grim and Gruesome
Sinister, Strange and Supernatural
Spooks, Spooks, Spooks
Thrillers, Chillers and Killers
Terrors, Torments and Traumas
Weirdies, Weirdies, Weirdies
Witches, Witches, Witches

MYSTERIOUS MENACING & MACABRE

AN ANTHOLOGY BY

HELEN HOKE

BOOKSALE

ELSEVIER/NELSON BOOKS
New York

No character in this book is intended to represent any actual person; all the incidents of the stories are entirely fictional in nature.

LIBRARY OF CONGRESS CATALOGING IN PUBLICATION DATA

Main entry under title:
Mysterious, menacing & macabre.
Contents: Side bet / Will F. Jenkins—"Happy birthday, dear Alexa" / John Keir Cross—The tombling day / Ray Bradbury—Head man / Robert Bloch—[etc.]
1. Horror tales, American. 2. Horror tales, English. 3. Children's stories, American. 4. Children's stories, English. [1. Horror stories. 2. Short stories]
I. Hoke, Helen, 1903– . II. Title: Mysterious, menacing, and macabre.
PZ5.M988 1981 [Fic] 81-9738
ISBN 0-525-66753-9 AACR2

ACKNOWLEDGMENTS

The selections in this book are used by permission of and special arrangements with the proprietors of their respective copyrights, who are listed below. The editor's and publisher's thanks go to all who have made the collection possible.

The editor and publisher have made every effort to trace ownership of all material contained herein. It is their belief that the necessary permissions from publishers, authors, and authorized agents have been obtained in all cases. In the event of any questions arising as to the use of any material, the editor and publisher express regret for any error unconsciously made and will be pleased to make the necessary corrections in future editions of the book.

"Dark Dream," by Elizabeth Fancett. From the *9th Fontana Book of Great Horror Stories.* Reprinted by permission of the author.

"The Demon Lover," by Elizabeth Bowen. From *The Demon Lover,* published by Jonathan Cape Ltd. Reprinted by permission of the Estate of Elizabeth Bowen and Jonathan Cape Ltd. Copyright 1946 and renewed 1974 by Elizabeth Bowen. Reprinted from *The Collected Stories of Elizabeth Bowen,* by permission of Alfred A. Knopf, Inc.

"Happy Birthday, dear Alex," by John Keir Cross. From *London Tales of Terror.* Reprinted by permission of the Estate of the late John Keir Cross by arrangement with A. M. Heath & Company, Ltd.

"Head Man," by Robert Bloch. Copyright 1950 by Popular Publications, Inc. Reprinted by permission of the author and the author's agents., Scott Meredith Literary Agency, Inc., 845 Third Avenue, New York, NY 10022.

"The Shuttered Room," by H. P. Lovecraft. From *The Shuttered Room and Other Tales of Terror,* by H. P. Lovecraft and August Derleth. Reprinted by permission of Arkham House Publishers, Inc., Sauk City, Wisconsin.

"Side Bet," by Will F. Jenkins. Copyright 1937 by the Crowell-Collier Publishing Company. Reprinted by permission of the author and the author's agents, Scott Meredith Literary Agency, Inc., 845 Third Avenue, New York, NY 10022.

To Opal, with Love

CONTENTS

Mysterious, Menacing & Macabre

ABOUT THIS BOOK

THE STORIES IN *Mysterious, Menacing, and Macabre* were chosen for the agreeable shudders it is hoped they will induce among the countless readers who relish such tales. Here, then, for the horrorphile are more fine works by some very popular writers—Ray Bradbury, Robert Bloch, and Roald Dahl being just three of the well-known stars in the firmament of supernatural and horror writing.

The tales are shrouded with an eerie, at times hazy, atmosphere that is suitable for their nature, but the punch is to be found in their masterful and unexpected conclusions. As your sensibilities feast on plot after deliciously terrifying plot, you will find each story diverse in its degree of horror.

In the ghastly situations depicted, you will often perceive a warning shadow. For instance, a signal of impending danger may be given by the low growling of a faithful, smart dog, as is done in the story "Two Spinsters." Here is a dangerous case in which swift counteraction may be possible. On the other hand, a portentous vision such as that experienced in sleep by the young wife in "Dark Dream" may be the mysterious manifestation of a situation that becomes a poignant and inherent part of her waking life.

There are times, however, where not even the slightest hint of menace is suggested. You will, therefore, have to wait for the very end of "Happy Birthday, Dear Alexa" to find out what happened to the cousin who scoured dingy shops in a dusky part of London for a special and awful birthday gift.

Unlike the man above, the "Head Man" is explicitly warned. A hapless victim of the terrible Nazi regime threatens this grim German executioner with the words, "As ye sow, so shall ye reap." You will gasp and shiver at the way ironic retribution goes to work as the prophecy is being ignored.

On the menacing side, "The Shuttered Room" is a haunting story of what happens when a young man returns to his homestead and uncovers a dreadful family secret. However, in the bone-chilling story, "The Way Up to Heaven," there is certainly no suggestion of menace on poor Mrs. Foster's part, whose misery is maliciously exploited by her husband.

Macabre is one way to describe "The Tombling Day." Thanks to its utterly strange climax, this weirdly humorous story is one that may well quicken your steps, particularly should you recall it while dancing!

The above are but a sampling of the horrific ingredients that nestle in the pages of this anthology, in the hope of whetting your appetite for a terrific banquet: the ambience is chilling; *every* story is par for the course.

Helen Hoke

SIDE BET

Will F. Jenkins

THERE WAS A vast blue bowl which was the sky. Across it, with agonizing slowness, there marched a brazen sun which poured down light to dazzle and burn out the man's eyes, and heat to broil the brains in his skull. At intervals the blue bowl grew dark and was dotted with stars, which ranged themselves in pairs like the eyes of a snake—unwinking and cold and maliciously amused—and watched through the night while the man recovered strength to endure the torture of another day. There was a sea of infinite blueness, which heaved slowly up and down and up and down and alternately reflected the blue bowl and the monstrous aggregation of star eyes. And there was the island, which was not more than fifty by fifteen yards in extent.

Also, there was the rat, with which the man played a game with rather high stakes, a game in which life was a side bet.

The man and the rat were not friends. No. When huge waves flung the man scornfully upon the island, he thought himself the sole survivor of his ship, and for twenty-four hours he disregarded every other thought or observation in trying to salvage as much of the wreckage as he could. He could not do much. During all that day and night colossal combers beat upon the shore, overwhelming two thirds of its length in sputtering spume. There was then no sky or sea or any other thing but hurtling masses of water and foam plunging upon and over and past the island. And the island was only rock. There was no vegetation. There was no shelter. There was barely more than a foothold behind a steep upcropping of wet and slippery stone. But now and again some fragment of the ship was pounded senselessly upon that upcrop by the sea, and the man tried desperately to salvage it.

He saved but little. A dozen crates of fruit broke open and all their contents went to waste upon rockery so continuously wave-swept as to be past clinging to. Four separate times he saw masses of cargo—some of which must have been edible—surge past the island, infuriatingly near yet impossibly distant. And a life raft, floating high in the water, was deliberately smashed and maliciously pounded before his eyes into splintered wood and crumpled metal—and then the sea took that away too.

Before the waves abated the man made sure of some bits of wood and some cordage, and from the life raft as it went to pieces he rescued a keg of water and a canvas bag of hard sea bread—biscuit. But there was nothing on which he could hope to leave the island, nor canvas to make a shelter, and he had not even a stick long enough to make a mast on which to fly his confession of helplessness and distress for the sea to look at.

But he did have a companion: the rat.

The rat was huge. It was a wise and resourceful ship rat and had all the cunning and ferocity of its race. Its body was almost a foot long. It had come ashore without help from the man; he never knew how. Perhaps clinging man-fashion to one of the two masses of spars and cordage now lodged securely on the island. But it had reached the island and it knew of the man's presence, and it knew exactly what the island offered of sustenance when the seas went down and the long, agonizing procession of days began in which the sky was a vast blue bowl and a brazen sun marched slowly across it.

When that happened, the man took account of his prospects, which were not bright. He counted his stores. He had twenty-two biscuits, all tainted with salt water, and a small keg of fresh water. There was a fairly impressive mass of lumber, mostly splintered and none suitable for the manufacture of a raft even if the man had possessed tools, which he did not. There was some rope, attached to shattered spars. In a money belt, the man had sixty dollars. That was all.

He had no matches, but he found that with a small spike extracted from the wreckage he could strike a spark from the rock of the island. He had nothing to cook, and therefore a fire was needless. But he picked cordage into oakum for tinder, and he arranged his stock of wood in a great pyre, the smaller splinters lowest, so that from a single spark he could send up a roaring beacon of flame and smoke to summon any ship he might sight from the island. His stock of food and water was so trivial that he rationed himself strictly. He could not actually live on such infinitesimal portions as he allotted himself for each day, but he would starve very slowly. He would live longer and suffer longer. The will to live is not a matter of reason. And then the days of waiting began as separate Gehennas of heat and thirst and hopelessness.

The sun by day was horrible. There was no shade. There was no shelter. There was no soil. There was only fissured, tumbled rock. The man scorched, panting in the baking heat, and gazed with smarting eyes at the horizon. He looked for a ship, though he could not really hope for one. In the morning he ate his strictly allotted ration, drank a very little water, and during the night he gathered strength to suffer through another day. From the amount of food and drink he possessed, he had calculated exactly how long he could live upon the island. He did not ask himself why he should wish to.

It was probably the seventh or eighth day when he learned that the rat was also on the island.

He had picked up the canvas bag which held the sea biscuits.

It should have been nearly full. His daily ration was small. But as he lifted the bag, something fell at his feet. There was a hole in the bag. A fine white powder sifted out of it, spreading in the air. At his feet was half a biscuit, irregularly gnawed. The tooth marks were clearly those of a rat.

The man's heart tried to stop. He regarded the hole and the gnawed biscuits with a sort of stupefied horror. Then he swiftly counted the contents of the bag. He should have had nineteen biscuits. Instead he had sixteen and the fragment, which was less than a half. More than a week of life had been taken from him.

He had no real hope of rescue, of course. The island was a speck in a waste of sea. It might or might not be on the charts. He did not know. If it was charted, ships would avoid it as a danger to navigation. But the instinct to cling to life is too strong for mere reason to controvert. The man's hands shook. He carefully unraveled a strand of rope. He tied up the hole in the bag. And he had apportioned his supplies to keep him alive for a certain number of days. He could not bring himself to surrender one hour of that scheduled time. Since a part of his food had been taken from him, he desperately resolved to cut down his ration to make up for the theft. And he did.

He chewed the reduced fraction of sea biscuit, which was his daily food, with exhaustive care. He made it last a very long time. He watched the horizon with dazzled, reddened eyes. He was already hungry all the time. He had hunger cramps in the night. His knees felt oddly exhausted when he climbed about the wave-rounded mass which was the island, but he resolutely made the journey. He watched all day. He saw nothing. When night came he drank the few swallows he allowed himself. He tied the bag to a spliced stick and propped it up so that it hung in midair. He slept.

In the morning the bag was on the ground again. The rat had gnawed through the cord upholding it. There were only twelve biscuits left, and the man saw a floury scraping on the rock, two yards from the bag, which told him that the rat had carried off one biscuit uneaten.

The man knew hatred now. And he made a savage search of every square inch of the island. It was not difficult. One hundred and fifty feet in one direction. About forty-five in another. Nothing of any size could hide, but there were cracks and crevices and miniature caverns in which the rat could conceal himself during the search. The man found one tiny, crumby place, where the rat had eaten, at leisure, food which was more than the man allowed himself for three days. And he came to have an inkling of how the rat drank. Even now, the small crevices in the rocks were cool. Undoubtedly moisture condensed upon their surfaces during the night and the rat licked it. It would serve a rat, but no man could live that way.

But he did not find the rat. He did not even catch a glimpse of it, but by this time he hated it with an emotion far past any hatred men ordinarily know.

That night the man's rage kept him from sleeping. He had a section of splintered plank not too heavy to be a club. He put out the bag of biscuits as bait and sat on guard beside it. The sun sank. The vast blue bowl turned dark and very many pairs of malevolent stars shone out, to look down upon him and watch him maliciously. His hands shook with hatred. The sea soughed and gurgled among the irregular rocks about the shoreline. The man waited, hating. . . .

But he was very weak. He woke suddenly. His club, held ready, had fallen with a crash to the rock before him. The sound had roused him. He heard the scurrying of tiny feet. The rat, scuttling away.

The canvas bag was a good two feet from where it had been. The rat had been trying to drag it to its own hiding place.

The man made inarticulate noises of fury. He knew, now, that the rat would seek to prey upon him for food as long as the two of them lived upon the island. That is the instinct of rats. And in any case he would have tried to kill the rat if he saw it, because that is the instinct of men. But here the conflict of instincts became more than inevitable. It became deadly. Both the man and the rat could not live upon this island. If the man lived, the rat died. If the man died, the chance of the rat for survival would be directly and specifically increased.

But the man was too weak to think very clearly. He had found a rock with a hollow in it. He put the bag of biscuits there and lay down. The rat could not reach the biscuits without first gnawing the man. But the man slept fitfully and even through his dreams there moved a hazy, groping thought. The rat must die, or he must. . . .

In the morning the man chewed his ration for hours. It was the fraction of a sea biscuit. He savored every particle of flavor it possessed. The heat beat upon him. He panted, watching the unchanging horizon beneath a brazen sun. He kept his body wetted with seawater so that he would not need to drink. But already he suffered severely from thirst. And then, toward nightfall, he saw the rat.

It was swimming toward an outlying rock which was perhaps ten yards from the main island. The rock was certainly no more than five feet across and rose perhaps that much above the slow, smooth swells which forever swayed across the sea.

The rat reached the base of that rock. It swam about it, trying to find gripping places for its paws. The man watched in a passion of sheer hatred until it disappeared. Then he moved closer. He heard its paws scratching and scrambling, out of sight. Presently its pointed muzzle appeared on top of the small rock. It went sniffing here and there. Suddenly it stopped stock-still. It began to eat. And the man smelled something tainted. Perhaps a dead fish flung to the top of the rock by a wave or swell. Perhaps a gull or tern which had died there recently. Whatever it was, the rat ate it.

The man trembled all over with hatred. He could no longer compute the anguish he had suffered, of hunger with but a tantalizing morsel of food a day, and of thirst with but enough of lukewarm water barely to moisten his lips. But the rat had enough of water, somehow, and now it fed!

The man stumbled back to his utterly useless cache of

shattered timbers and weathered cordage. He thought bitterly of the rat's smooth body. Of its unshrunken muscles. Of its sleek fur. And suddenly, as in his hatred he envisioned rending it limb from limb—suddenly he saw it in a new light. From a thing to be hated and destroyed, the rat suddenly became a fascinating, an infinitely desirable thing. The man was starving. As he thought of the rat, his mouth watered.

The conditions of the game now were wholly clear. If the man died, the rat's chances of survival would be directly increased. If the rat died, the man would live longer at least by days. So the rat must die, or the man. They had played a deadly game before. Now the side bet—of life—was explicit.

Days passed. The sun rose and there was a vast blue bowl which was the sky. The sun sank and a multitude of stars gazed down. The man gave all his thought, now, to the game. He did not even glance at the horizon. He grew rapidly weaker, but his whole thought was fixed upon the construction of elaborate gins and traps by which the rat might be captured. He made them, and they failed, because he could not bring himself to risk even a scrap of food for bait.

Then he made a bow and arrow. It was clumsy and crude, and it would be hopelessly inaccurate, because he had no tools. When he had made the weapon, he spent three days stalking the rat over the uneven surface of the island. Most of the time he had to crawl, because of his weakness. Much of the time he knew where the rat was. Some of the time he even saw it, because the rat had grown bolder since the man's weakness had forced him to crawl rather than walk.

The first day's stalking brought no results. Nor the second. But on the third day—even the rat was starving now—the man's persistence and infinite care took him to where he saw the rat clearly. It was sleeping. The man crept closer, inch by inch. He moved with breathless caution. He saw, though he did not realize, that the rat's ribs now showed through its fur. Its eyes were rimmed with red. It was no longer sleek and well-muscled.

It was shabby and unkempt and almost as emaciated as the man.

The man drew his solitary arrow back. But he had not realized his weakness. His heart pounded hysterically. His eyes glared. His mouth slobbered in horrible anticipation. His hands shook. And when he had drawn back the arrow to the fullest extent of which he was capable, the arrow flicked forward, glanced off a rock—it would have missed—and by sheer ironic accident was deflected again into its true path. It struck the rat.

And the bow had been drawn so weakly that the arrow did not penetrate. The rat leaped upright, squeaking, and fled. And the useless arrow lay where it had fallen while the starving man wept. He saw, now, that it was the rat which would win the game and the stakes—and the side bet.

The rat knew it, too. Two days later the man's rations, both of food and water, came to an end. He regarded them both for a long time. Once gone, the rat would win their deadly game.

The man ate the bread and drank the water. He lay down. He did not bother even to glance at the horizon, because the game was over and he had lost. He was not suffering at all when night came. He felt no hunger and even his thirst was not severe. He was peculiarly clearheaded and calm. His body was weak, to be sure, but there were no gripings in his belly. He lay and looked up at the stars and foresaw the rat's winning of game and stakes and side bet, and was unmoved by the foreknowledge. He was too weak for emotion.

But then he heard a little sound, and in the starlight he saw a movement. It was the rat.

It was still for a long time. The man did not move. It crept toward him. The man stirred. The rat stopped. Presently it sank down on all fours, watching the man with glowing eyes.

There was silence save for the gurgling of the long, slow swells among the rocks. The man even laughed weakly. The rat waited with a quivering impatience. It had known nothing of rationing. It had eaten more fully than the man, but not as often. Its whole body was a clamoring, raging hunger. It quivered with a horrible desire to claim its winnings in the deadly game.

"No," said the man detachedly. His voice was a bare croak, but there was almost amusement in it. "Not yet! The one who dies first loses. I'm not dead yet. . . ."

The rat quivered. It backed away when the man spoke, its eyes flaring hatred. But when he stopped it crept forward. A little closer than before. It stopped only when the man stirred.

Then the man thought of something. He was very weak indeed, but at the very beginning he had picked out some soft fiber from the cordage he had saved. He had worked out a small spike, and he tested it against the rock. He had even dried out a little seaweed, as more practical than hemp for the making of a blaze.

Now he struck the spike against the rock. It sparked. The rat retreated. Presently it crept forward again. The man struck the spike again upon the rock. The rat was checked.

It happened many times before the sparks struck in the improvised oakum tinder. Then it fatigued the man very much to blow it and sift dried and crumpled seaweed upon it—blowing the while—and later to transfer the small coal to the assembly of little splinters he had made ready long since. They were to kindle the signal fire he had intended to light if a ship should ever come into view. But now he lighted the kindling because the rat was no more than five feet from him and he could hear it panting in a desperate eagerness to claim its winnings. The flames caught and climbed.

The rat drew back slowly, his eyes desperate. The man watched.

Over his head malicious stars looked down, but now a huge and spreading column of smoke rose up, lighted from below by the blaze. It blotted out the stars. And the flames climbed higher and higher, crackling fiercely, and the fire roared. There was a leaping thicket of yellow flame beneath the smoke. Its topmost branches reared up for fifteen feet. Twenty. Long tongues of detached incandescence licked up into the thick smoke even higher still. And the reddish-yellow glare upon the smoke made it into a radiant mist.

It would have been a pretty good signal, the man thought.

Then he thought of something else. If he could have contrived to be upon that heap of blazing timber, and had contrived that it should catch fire after he was dead, the rat would never collect its winnings from the game.

"But that wouldn't have been fair," said the man lightheartedly. "It, it would've been welshing. . . ."

The rat vanished, crept into some crack or crevice to hide from the glare and the heat of the fire. And the fire blazed up and up, and slowly died down, and when the dawn came the man saw smoke still rising from the ashes.

And again he saw the rat.

But he heard—he heard the rattle of an anchor chain. It was that of a ship that had seen the flame-lit smoke of the fire during the dark hours, had thought it another ship ablaze, and had come to offer help. Now the boat was on its way ashore.

When they carried the man to the small boat, he croaked out a request. They placed him as he wished in the boat, so that as it pulled toward the ship he saw the island. And he saw the rat upon it.

The rat ran crazily back and forth, squealing. The squeals were cries of rage. The rat was a bare skeleton covered with tight-stretched hide, and its rage was ghastly. Its disappointment was incredible. The man was being carried away, and there was no other food upon the island.

"I—I've got a money belt on," croaked the man. "There's sixty dollars in it. I . . . I've lost a bet." He rested for a moment. "I want to buy some food and have it left on the island for that . . . rat. He won the game from me and I . . . don't want to welsh on a bet. . . ."

They lifted him carefully to the steamer's deck. Weakly, he insisted on this final favor. The boat went back to the island. It left a great heap of more than a hundred pounds of ship's biscuits where the sea was not likely to wash any of it away. Before it had pulled out from the island, the rat had flung itself upon the heap and was eating.

They told the man. He grinned feebly . . . he had been fed . . . and went incontinently to sleep. They told him afterward that the rat was still eating when the ship sailed over the horizon.

What happened after that, the man never knew. But he felt that he had paid the side bet.

"HAPPY BIRTHDAY, DEAR ALEXA"

John Keir Cross

I AM, ESSENTIALLY, I think, a simple man.

I make the statement with no kind of false modesty: it is only something that has become apparent as my long life has gone on and I have failed so often, until it is too late, to comprehend the small complexities with which we are all surrounded from day to day.

I shall even be simple in setting down this particular incident in my life— I shall have no skill in any kind of storytelling about it, and so you will see through it all long before I may reach a particular point which someone more skillful in the art of writing would have been able to mask for dramatic effect. You will see through Hare's terrible secret from the start, I daresay, where I never did till it all was almost over.

His shop was in a small side street. From the start I should perhaps have suspected something sinister from the very air and atmosphere of the place, yet naturally, on such a quest, one hardly expected anything other than a slightly unusual flavor, shall I say. Certainly the other shops I had previously visited were also peculiar in one way or another, even the one that was very large and medicated in Marylebone. No doubt the association from the commodity I was seeking predisposed one to subjective impressions somewhat macabre.

The commodity in question was to be a gift for my young cousin, Alexa. It was, in fact, to be a birthday gift—how strange a birthday gift!—yet one that would be curiously welcome. One hardly quite knew where to begin—it is, after all, not the kind of gruesome relic that one is likely to wish to purchase every day; one had certainly no realization that there was even a positive shortage of the articles, with consequent visions of patient queues of earnest students assembled outside a supplier momentarily well stocked. But it all was so; and after a while there came even to be a sense of mild excitement in the quest, as source after source was explored unavailingly, yet more and more clues were uncovered as to possible further milieux for inquiry. . . .

You will note, no doubt—I realize it myself reading back this laborious opening of mine (laborious since, as I have said, I am no skilled writer)—that I have, probably from some lingering sense of delicacy, so far avoided any open mention by name of the commodity's nature. Let me come to it boldly and straightly, then: the object I sought to purchase was none other than a human skeleton! And the explanation for the horrid search is simplicity itself—as again you will plainly have guessed: my cousin was a medical student, engaged conscientiously in a meditation upon the mysteries of anatomy. . . .

I do not exaggerate, incidentally, when I say that at the period of which I write so inexpertly, the objects in question were in great demand and short supply. I had even read a mildly humorous article in *The Times* not long before to that very effect—one of the inimitable fourth leaders of that notable journal which still, behind a façade of some lightheartedness, announced the undoubted fact that for one reason or another, skeletons for medical study purposes had become extremely difficult to obtain, and those that were available, even at third or fourth hand, as their owners progressed beyond the necessity of further study, were outside the purses of most young medicos. It was where I thought I might be of some assistance; Alexa had been in the search for some time, only to find that indeed the prices were outrageous, where I, more fortunately endowed with this world's goods through a pleasing inheritance some years previously, might be able to be of some worthwhile family assistance—and with Alexa's birthday not far in the offing, might also (if the mild jest may be permitted) kill two birds, as it were, with one somewhat costly stone.

My first difficulty, however, was to know even where to begin, as I think I have already stated. But by dint of some discreet inquiry among medical friends—even of Alexa during a supposedly social visit only—I eventually found myself on the long trail, calling one bright spring morning at that large and distinguished-looking shop in Marylebone.

I was interviewed by a young man of superior smartness, with a curiously clean and—if I may say so—a sterile look. As I moved forward to confront him, I found myself almost slipping on the excessively polished linoleum beneath my feet. All around me were glistening machines and implements of unknown medical functionalism—trays and boxes of neat cold forceps, curiously shaped scissors, small knives, contrivances spouting arrays of red rubber tubings. At the back, where the light—perhaps fortunately—was somewhat shady, there were some shelves of silent bottles, with nameless shapes afloat in their spirituous depths. About the whole place was an elusive odor of linoleum polish and formalin. I found myself oppressed, but the thought of young Alexa's forthcoming pleasure sustained me.

The assistant inclined a somewhat oleaginous but courteous head, with a murmured request that I should state my requirement.

"I want," I began, with some initial nervousness, "I want to purchase—ah—not for myself, you understand—for a friend—a cousin, in fact . . . I—ah—had wanted to inquire about the possibility of obtaining—"

At that moment, as I glanced somewhat timidly about me, I saw, calmly regarding me from a small pedestal, a prime specimen of the object of my very search. The disinterested glare of the hollow orbs unnerved me a little, then I was able to give a small exclamation of satisfaction as I gestured toward it.

"A skeleton, sir?" The young man's tone held a trace, I thought, of professional sorrow—as if, almost, I were a near relative of the deceased we both now contemplated, swaying a little on its suspending wires. I remember reflecting, even in the moment, how unexpectedly small we are untrammeled at last by flesh—those little spindly bones of ours, so frail-seeming against the might of the world: the perpetual grin of our hapless mouths behind whatever expression of grief or soft sentiment our lips might once have worn; our dry small cage of a chest enclosing hearts that once throbbed deliriously in joy or passion; our boxy little skulls within whose confines noble thoughts may once have raced, whole symphonies or epics been composed, the plans of great cathedrals limned. . . . So went my simple thoughts, until I became aware that the young man was still speaking in his smoothly modulated way:

"Articulated, of course?"

"Of course," I nodded. Unacquainted with the terminologies, I assumed that the expert before me must have some profound purposes in his "of course." Besides, I recollected Alexa having said something, too, about this need for "articulation" in the article.

"Somewhat in this manner, perhaps," went on the young man gravely, stepping forward toward our solitary companion and touching a wire stretched almost invisibly along the spine.

Instantly, with a small dry rustling—hardly more than a whisper through the antiseptic silence—He Who Once Had Been executed a deft brief convulsion of all his members, simultaneously. He quivered and revolved with a delicate waving of arms, an inclination of legs, a pointing of slender toes. He engaged in a total arabesque, a chilly mechanical ecstasy of interrelated bones and silver pivotal pins, through all his tiny joints . . . and, as I started back a little, involuntarily apprehensive, the young man beside me said reverentially, in such a tone as I might once have used myself in my distant youth in a contemplation of Madame Pavlova, no less:

"Beautiful—ah, beautiful! Such poise, such balance, sir—such exquisite coordination!"

Then, with a further humble moment before the great dancer now slowly settling to no more than a lingering wavy tremor, he turned to me suddenly, briskly.

"I'm sorry, sir—deeply sorry. We are quite out of stock."

"Nothing at all?" I asked, as one might ask in the normal course of day-to-day shopping when confronted with a shortage of, say, summer shirtings during the holiday season or warm underwear with the approach of winter.

"Nothing, sir. Our supplies are very limited—the demand of late has been quite remarkable."

"To what," I asked academically, "do you attribute such a curious state of—" I had almost said "trading," then changed to " 'shortage in this line'?"

"It is difficult to say, sir. At one time we carried almost more of the articles in our stockrooms than we had space for—we frequently had to dismember them entirely so as to be able to find accommodation; for, as you will understand, it is an easier matter to group, say, all the tibiae, all the fibulae, in one shelf, with all the metacarpals in another, and so forth, than to pack the fully assembled items together with any . . . well . . . comfort."

(I groped a little at his undoubtedly strange use of the word "comfort," visualizing that unimaginable stockroom somewhere below and far away—beyond the shady bottles on the farther shelves, perhaps. . . .)

"You haven't, by any chance—" and I hesitated again, wondering how one might convey the possibility of an under-the-counter purchase, recollecting one's wartime habits in the acquiring of tobacco or whiskey, for example.

"Nothing at all, sir," he said severely. "We think sometimes that it may all be due to the Health Service in some indefinable way—no doubt that people are living longer, perhaps—"

"No doubt," I said vaguely.

"—or even that patients are tending to die in their beds rather than in the unnamed wards of hospitals. We had some useful connections in the better times with the riverside morgues, for instance; but somehow suicides are less frequent than they were—or rather, should I say, the present-day practitioners tend to stay at home rather more. The genial sleeping-draft overdose has come somewhat to the fore; and so one is more in the position of being found by relatives or friends and given—as they say—a decent burial."

He contrived to inject an odd flavor of distaste and even disapproval into his tone.

"These things move in trends, of course," he concluded with a sigh. "One can hardly predict or even comprehend the general movements in trade. And it was never, of course, the kind of commodity that could be . . . well, as one might say . . . made to measure. It is hardly a case for the assembly line."

"Plastics?" I murmured tentatively, with visions of a fortune to be made in a factory established somewhere in the Midlands, the young men and women streaming to work each morning on bicycles, the staff canteens, the Sports Welfare Clubs, the whole great machinery of modern industry geared toward meeting the strange demand. Yet I realized in an instant that I had made an immense faux pas. He regarded me with an ill-concealed pity.

"It would hardly perhaps serve, sir. In our profession we must observe the proprieties. We are dealing, I think, with Fundamentals. Plastics would be hardly . . . well . . . worthy, shall I say?"

There remained one more possibility. Small as he had made me feel, I said boldly, with a somewhat forlorn gesture, "Perhaps—perhaps that model there—?"

He froze to an immobility as marked as that of the now still subject of our whole discourse.

"I beg your pardon, sir! It is for exhibition only. It has been with us since the initial establishment of our whole business. It is in fact—and was bequeathed as such, so that, as he put it in his will, he might constantly be in a position to watch our progress—it is, in fact, our original Founder. . . . Good morning, sir: I am sorry not to have been able to have been of more assistance."

I crept into the bright sunshine. With one backward apologetic glance I saw him stare after me with an expression of supreme distaste on his face. I could have sworn, in the shadows there, that he then turned for a moment and bowed to that small dangling shape that once had trotted so briskly, so joyously, through the very medicated doorway from which I had that instant emerged. . . . I told you, I think, that I was—and indeed am—an unsophisticated man. . . .

I will not weary you with a full account of my peregrinations. At every turn I met only frustration. I visited shops of a like nature to, but less opulent than, that veritable temple in Marylebone. But the tale was constantly the same—a hundred assistants, some sympathetic, some brusque, some positively rude, announced the identical dismal state of affairs. Skulls—yes, occasionally; isolated tibiae or fibulae, possibly; complete feet more rarely, but still at least remotely; pelvises—by some strange freak, pelvises by the score; but fully articulateds?—no, sir! One very aged proprietor of a small supplier off Holborn told me gloomily, being more courteous than most dealers that I encountered, "I've been in the trade, man and boy, sir, for sixty years and more; and I've known nothing like it, nothing, not since the days of the great 'Uman 'Eart shortage in '02.' "

"And what was that?" I enquired, offering him a cigar, which he took with some absence of mind, his eyes fixed nostalgically on that distant past.

"Terrible times, sir, terrible. In the old days we done quite a trade on the side in 'Uman 'Earts—'Aitch-Aitches' as we used to call 'em. Pickled 'em in acid and such and used to put 'em up in handy little jars that we bought wholesale from the jam factory down the road—(changed the labels, o'course). You won't remember them old times of the Pawning Days?"

I shook my head. By this time, you will comprehend, I had acquired a positive interest, if not a thorough fascination, for the whole subject. The Pawning Days—the unimaginable Pawning Days!

"When you was down and out," said my informant, leaning confidentially over a counter littered with secondhand syringes, scalpels, tweezers, stethoscopes, and the like, "—which I don't suppose you've never been in all your life, sir, nor never hope to . . . but when you was down and out in them old days, and you'd pawned your watch and your overcoat and your spare elastic-sideds and such, and the old rolled gold medallion with your mother's picture inside and a lock of hair, there was still one thing left that you could pawn, and it was yourself."

"Yourself," I said noncommittally.

"Yourself, sir. You went into St. William's 'Orspital, like, and you said, 'Ere I am, what's left of me.' And they said, 'Good, sign here.' And they gave you a form, sir, and it said on it that in exchange for a five-pun note you hereby bequeathed your body to medical science for research when such time should arrive as you passed on, see. Now, if you signed another form which said as you'd never smoked or had a drink and never would, then you got another fiver, and that made ten. So off you went with your cash, see, and that was you fixed. But if times got better for you—if you maybe came into a fortune or such—you could always go and get yourself out again: and if you were a five-pound job that would cost eight, see, 'cos they had to have their profit, but if you was a ten-pounder it was eighteen, 'cos they reckoned that if you didn't smoke and didn't drink they'd have to wait anyways, and so the interest was higher, like. But there wasn't many as was able to redeem themselves that way, and so they was the great times for Aitch-Aitches, and skeletons too, see."

"And what happened in '02 to put an end to it all?" I asked.

"Reckon the 'Orspitals got wise to it, see. 'Cos after St.

William's started it, every other 'Orspital ran a scheme too. And there was chaps that made a regular living out of going round 'em all and signing papers right, left, and center, so that when the time came nobody knew what tibia belonged to who and what fibula belong to t'other. So in '02 they all stopped simultaneous, and there we were—not an Aitch-Aitch in the place, there weren't."

He stayed gloomily contemplating that terrible period of slump, then shook himself.

"Ah, well, times picked up a bit after all, in the 20's, I s'pose, 'cos of the fashionable suicide wave, see; but now they've settled back again, now that folks are more home-keeping and we've the Health Service and such—" And in his more homely way he repeated the curious argument of my supercilious friend of Marylebone.

I left him at last with a desolate conviction that the day would never come when I would be able to provide poor Alexa with a birthday present—particularly with that birthday looming constantly nearer and nearer. He gave me only one word of possible comfort:

"Take my advice, sir, and don't go 'round the medical suppliers. We're all in the same boat, see. Pawnshops—that's the ticket."

"Pawnshops?"

"Yes, sir—them or the secondhand lads down side streets. You see, the only time one of Them-There comes on the market is when some young student chap like this cousin of yours you was telling me about gets hard up sudden-like. So they round the corner to Uncle with What's-'Is-Name slung over their shoulder, and that's good for a tenner, you know, 'cos with things as they are, Uncle can sell 'em again for as much as thirty or forty to chaps like you as is on the search, see. Mind you, mostly they're pretty old and falling to bits by the time they gets to Uncle, but even so, there's sometimes something young and tasty-like will turn up. So you just go on that tack, sir—there's a little shop in

Camberwell I can give you the address of, that's been running Them-Theres for quite a times as a speciality—if you mention my name he'll see you straight. . . ."

He gave me the address and I visited Camberwell. And so, eventually, the long trail drew toward its conclusion as I came in sight of Mr. Hare. . . .

—But not at first—not still for some little time. I had some further dismal rounds to perambulate. By this time the tension was rising within me to some positive degree of discomfort. The birthday was drawing closer and closer, yet still I saw little chance of success. And something else had arisen to occasion worry—something which might have held some element of the ludicrous were it not for the danger I saw in it that my whole scheme of a pleasant surprise for my young cousin might topple to desolate failure.

As I moved from shop to shop on my quest, I had sometimes been aware of occasional faces becoming increasingly familiar—mostly of young men standing beside me at the various counters awaiting their turn, or approaching them as I withdrew. From a muttered remark once overheard, it one day dawned on me that these were none other than seekers like myself—young medicos who were also on the trail, chasing the elusive skeletons from shop to shop as I was. It was a simple step toward the further apprehensive thought that even Alexa might be searching among those others—that there was consequently a chance, however remote a chance, that I might be forestalled!

The consideration quite appalled me. With the final examinations comparatively near at hand, Alexa's need for a skeleton to study was growing quite imperative—it was why I had known from the first that my projected gift would be so singularly welcome to that studious cousin of mine. I had never disclosed my intention—in all gifts, I have always felt in my simple way, there should be an element of surprise. It was more than likely that in what little time could be spared from study, Alexa would be seeking to obtain the curious heart's desire I also sought—and if our paths should cross—!

I had veritable confirmation of the danger on the very day of my visit to the little shop in Camberwell that had been recommended by the friendly dealer in Holborn. At the very moment of my approach to it, I saw Alexa's familiar figure hurrying out!

I concealed myself in a convenient doorway, then made my own way forward. The shop was small and dark—a misery of ancient junk of every description, the entire stock piled high in the single evil-smelling room—great heaps of soiled clothes, piles of cracked crockery, broken tables, crooked chairs . . . but as far as I could see, no skeletons.

"No, sir," said the dealer gloomily, when I made my need known to him. "Not in two years I ain't seen one. Old Joe up Holborn way was right, though—used to deal in 'em regular. It's just that somehow they're so hard to come by now I've give it up."

"Tell me," I said hastily, "—that young student who came in a moment before me . . . I think I know the face. As a matter of interest—"

The dealer smiled before I had completed the very sentence.

"Exactly the same, sir," he said. "I was just thinking how queer it was. Wanted one o' Them-There too. In fact, there's several been in lately—might be worth my while to start up trade again, if I can even lay my hands on the stuff. Only thing is"—and he suddenly shrugged—"I doubt if it would even be worth it. These young folk these days hardly have a chance, have they?"

"Why?" I asked.

"Cash, see. Even if I got one or two in, I could hardly sell 'em under forty or forty-five smackers . . . and it ain't every younker of a student could lay hands on that amount of cash."

He was right, of course—and I saw a sudden ray of hope.

From my knowledge of Alexa's resources it was only too plain that the purchase would be quite out of the question. Whereas I had only to trace the one physical object—one single skeleton in reasonable repair and, of course, articulated—poor Alexa had to go further and find one at the very most costing ten or fifteen; and, with the demand as it plainly was, there was little likelihood of that.

I acquired a new confidence—yet still had a lingering far-off edge of apprehension. I sped from shop to shop—from Camberwell to Kentish Town, on an elusive trail thereafter to a pawnbroker in Cheapside who had been recommended—to a tangled junk yard in the Minories—to an aged surly crone almost invisible behind the piled-high horrors of a used-clothing store in Rotherhithe.

It was she who gave me, with some reluctance at first, an address in Pimlico—then suddenly, peering closely at me, cackled quite hideously as she repeated it.

I found the side street in a maze of crooked alleys and vennels behind Sloane Square—saw the name in blistered paintwork above the most wretched shop my eyes had ever confronted: "W. Hare, General Dealer." Having learned my lesson in Camberwell, I reconnoitered the neighborhood with some care for a possible sign of Alexa; then, satisfied, pushed forward and entered.

A cracked bell tinkled dismally through a musty dark silence. A small, withered creature wearing a black skullcap came forward from the shadows. I babbled my request in some haste, anxious to escape from the whole unpleasant place as quickly as I could. I had even turned to the door again, so conditioned had I become to constant bleak refusal. But suddenly my distaste for my surroundings was swallowed in a great wave of relief as I heard Hare's thin and melancholy voice: "Why, yes, sir. I think I might be able to accommodate you. If you will give me a few particulars, perhaps . . . ?"

For all his small repulsiveness I might almost in that exciting moment have embraced him!

He leaned closely to me across his piled counter. I perched as well as I could on a rachitic chair, which, although plainly set out for the convenience of customers, still bore a price ticket: seven-and-six.

With my eyes a little accustomed to the gloom, I found myself gazing into the most horrible face I have ever seen. It was itself, almost, a skull. The lips were thin and cracked, drawn in a perpetual rictus-grin from teeth that were totally black. The skin stretched yellowly across his high cheekbones was so taut as almost to seem transparent—there was a momentary horrid temptation to set out a finger to poke through it bloodlessly, as if it were parchment. The eyes were pale and curiously glazed, with no spark of life in them, hooded beneath crusted and rheumy lids. . . . The man was a living corpse.

And from him, or from the monstrous assembly of mysteries in that shop of his, there was a smell unconscionably repulsive. What its true nature was I had no notion—yet it was a condensation somehow of a smell I had encountered before: somehow animal—somehow associated with . . . with what? I am a simple man: perhaps, in that moment, if I had been a little more worldly-wise for all my years—however . . .

"You will realize," he was saying in his soft toneless voice, that it may take a day or two before I can lay my hands on a specimen. I have none in stock, as it happens—"

"How long?" I asked impatiently. With my first relief now over I was only anxious again to escape from the oppressive atmosphere of that dark and evil corner of London.

"A week, shall we say? I must negotiate with my contacts."

"A week! Great heavens, man," I almost shouted, "I can't wait a week! It's for a—"

Yet I hesitated. It seemed grotesque, suddenly, even in that place so grotesque itself, to announce that the object was required for a gift. I was mentally calculating dates—and realized that in all my general excitement I had had an impression of time more pressing than it actually was. A week from the fourth would be the eleventh—the very day itself of the birthday.

"You could guarantee it in a week?" I asked.

"Most certainly—indeed quite definitely, sir. Articulated, of course?"

"Articulated," I said.

"And—as to size? Would you require something on the larger side or the smaller, perhaps?"

The thing was absurd, of course. I could only stare at him for a moment. He spoke in his toneless way as a tailor might, discussing one's next suit. He had a small, much-fingered notebook on the counter before him—and held over it the grimed stub of a pencil in fingers quite hideously crooked, all marked and burned with strange yellow stains.

"It . . . it hardly matters," I said—somewhat lamely, I feel now—in something of an anticlimax after all my tension. My aim—my only aim—was to buy the thing: it was even absurd, after everything I had been through, to discover that there might be such a thing as a choice in the matter.

"I would suggest small, sir," he said smoothly, writing carefully. "They are somewhat easier for me to obtain—and are, of course, more portable. So. And male?—or female?"

Again, I could only stare. The choice was still more bizarre. Was there even any difference?—Alexa had never once suggested any kind of preference. Beyond a dim recollection of some Biblical lore about more or fewer ribs, I could not conceive of any vital reason why one sex should be more or less suitable for the purposes of study than the other.

He saw my hesitation and fluted quietly: "Then if I may suggest again, sir, female. They also are a little easier for me to obtain. And besides, in the thought of the more delicate flesh once enclosing them—"

He broke off his intolerable leer as he saw the expression on my face. I believe I might almost have struck him!

"You will require it packed, sir?" he asked, even a little hastily, turning the dangerous corner. "I have a consignment of suitable lightweight cardboard boxes I usually use for the purpose."

The very question of transport had never occurred to me. I had had a far notion, in the earlier days of the search, of an arrangement with Carter Paterson or some such firm of conveyors of general merchandise. I saw now that if I was collecting the gift on the very day I was also having to deliver it, I would have to remove it and transport it myself. Were such things heavy, I wondered?—would the box fit comfortably into a taxi?

Again it was as if he read my thoughts.

"You will find it very light and easily carried, sir. If I might suggest a taxicab when you call—?"

I nodded again and rose.

"Yes—packed, then," I said abruptly. "But I should like to examine it, of course, before I take it."

"Of course, sir. It was my intention. I shall have it ready a week from today, and it will be a matter of moments to enclose it in the box after your examination."

He smiled with a hollow malevolence and shut the notebook with a snap.

"And the price, sir? Shall we say . . . fifty?"

It was larger than I had anticipated, even knowing the general situation. But I could ill afford a hesitation this time, with the end so happily at last in sight.

"Very well. Fifty."

"Guineas, sir?"

"Guineas!"

"Thank you, sir. And if I may suggest it, since you will be taking the article away with you . . . cash, sir?—rather than a check?"

"Cash, Mr. Hare!"

"Thank you, sir. I feel quite certain that you will be completely satisfied. Good evening, sir. A week from today—at, shall we say, eleven o'clock in the morning, perhaps, if that is convenient?"

I left him bowing across the counter, his yellow hands clasped tightly, the tassel of his skullcap dangling over his thin hooked nose. I stumbled around silent heaps of rubbish—of monstrous vases set on pedestals, dead marble busts of no conceivable value, tall looming bric-a-brac stands in outmoded Victorian bamboo-work, poker-work, repulsively carved walnut. . . . Behind me the bell tinkled faintly as I achieved the blessed air away from the eternal smell and hurried from the shop as quickly as I could move. W. Hare—General Dealer!

It was the name, indeed, more than any other circumstance, that I found curiously lingering to haunt me. As the week passed by in a strange indolence after all the fury of my quest from that bare and antiseptic temple in Marylebone to the dingy horrors of the little shop in Pimlico, I found myself strangely repeating at odd moments simply: "W. Hare, W. Hare, W. Hare . . ." and seeking some elusive association—as elusive in its different way as the odor from the man which had so oppressed me. Yet whatever I might feel about his unpleasantness—his positive evil, indeed, as I recollected his whole essence in that dusky place, leaning forward over his notebook—whatever I might feel, I had also to recognize that the man had saved me. And in that thought, as the week went on, I regained some measure of delight. I had exaggerated—my simple mind had grown infected through its piling disappointments, through the half-ludicrous gruesomeness of the whole adventure. When I encountered Hare again in the clearer light of day, his warped grotesqueness would reveal itself only as something subjective creeping through my own mind in a consideration of the macabre nature of the goods purveyed. He was even, no doubt, a simple man like myself, of quiet tastes and lonely habits. . . .

On the eve, my excitement mounted to a pitch where I could not sleep. I lay tossing for some hours, reflecting on the pleasure I was to give next day. I took a mouthful of brandy, and when it after all did not have the soporific effect I usually expect from it, I turned to my bedside bookshelf for consolation from my favorite Dickens.

It was when I read the passages referring to the nefarious secret occupation of the good Jerry Cruncher in the immortal *Tale of Two Cities* that I suddenly, with a small mortal chill, recalled the association in the name of that "General Dealer" of mine in Pimlico. Jerry Cruncher the Resurrectionist—those other notorious real-life Resurrectionists in the old Edinburgh of a hundred and fifty years ago . . . Burke and Hare—Burke and *Hare* . . .

I almost laughed aloud in the suddenly realized folly of it all. The thing was a coincidence and an association, no more. Nevertheless, it made me lose for once my taste for the Master and I tossed the book aside, seizing instead another favorite—a volume of the enchanting short stories of the good O. Henry . . . and opening it by another coincidence—an altogether happier one—at that famous little masterpiece, "The Gift of the Magi."

In its lulling sentimental influence I fell asleep at last and woke to a bright and cheerful morning, all horror vanished.

The mood still lingered as I directed my cabdriver to the little street in Pimlico. Indeed and indeed my fears and imaginings had been the merest shadows! The very shop in the bright sunlight was almost cheerful in its ridiculous window display of old rugs and tarnished silverware, its shelves of outspread books at threepence and sixpence per volume. I entered it blithely, determined against any recurrence of the old oppression, and found Hare already awaiting me, his hands, as always, clasped before him, his skullcap tassel dangling.

The smell was still about me, but I hardly noticed it—was determined at least to ignore it. There was little time, indeed, to notice anything in the sudden contemplation in that magic moment of the object at last of all my searching—for there, set against the end of the counter, was the beautiful thing itself!

And you know, in a curious way it even was quite beautiful to me at that moment, even apart from all the pleasure of its finding, the further pleasure it would give. In *itself* it had a strange beauty—the slightly yellowed bones so cunningly fitted, the gleam here and there of the tarnished silver articulation pins and wires. Not the face, perhaps—or the lack of face: a skull can never be beautiful . . . but somehow the whole marvelous framework of it, once the supports of the very uttermost marvel of all God's universe!

The dealer had set it in one of those tall, specially made cardboard boxes of his, the lid of it waiting in readiness on the floor. He asked if I wished to examine the articulation more closely, but I shook my head—apart from my inexpertness, I knew at a glance that the thing was as perfect a specimen as could be obtained. I almost chuckled to little harmless Hare in my delight as he set to fitting the lid in position and tying the whole long parcel for me with white new string, strangely out of place in that shop of dingy secondhandness. I counted out the notes I had obtained from my bank on the way to Pimlico—found I had no ten-shilling notes and cheerfully, as Hare fumbled in a pocket for change, cried:

"Leave it so, Mr. Hare, at fifty-three! You deserve it!"

In its box the skeleton was smaller than it had even seemed before—I had a recurrence of my philosophic thoughts from Marylebone. And it was after all quite curiously light, as Hare had said— I could carry it with the greatest ease to the waiting taxi.

"I marked, sir," he said, as he opened his tinkling door for me, "a small *H* in pencil at the head end, so that you can keep it upright as you carry it, before unpacking. It will avoid damage to the articulation."

It was a small and friendly touch, I felt, and I smiled to him as he stooped in a final bow to me on the pavement.

The girl who lived with Alexa opened the door of the flat to me. She was an engaging, nubile young creature, I had always felt, named Miriam. I propped the box—head upward, of course—against the lintel, smiling at her, yet noticing, too, that she wore an unexpected worried look.

"Alexa isn't in," she said, and my triumphant moment vanished. I had built so carefully to it—so carefully! In my simplicity it had never occurred to me to confirm that my young cousin would be available to receive my gift. I had a thought to go away and come back—to ask if I might wait. It was essential that the presentation should be carried out by myself and not by proxy, after all that I had gone through. But Miriam was speaking again.

"It's been worrying me to death," she said. "Of course, we only live together, and I naturally can't be expected to be given a note of all Alexa's movements, but to have gone away for so long without a single word—"

She broke off almost petulantly, regarding me in the gloomy small corridor.

"For so long?" I asked, dazed a little.

"A week, nearly enough—and not a single word. It's *too* bad."

I wonder if I had my first inkling even then—in my simplicity.

I gestured rather lamely to the tall package.

"It was to have been . . . a birthday gift," I said desolately. Miriam smiled.

"Of course!—I'd forgotten the date! Alexa must surely come back home for that! Do you want to leave it?"

"Yes," I said. "I'll leave it."

I turned away. There was no other immediate emotion in me, I think, but a great detached sadness—over my own inability, through my simplicity, to comprehend after all the years the ironic bitterness of the bright world in which we live. I reflected, too, I believe, on the strangeness of coincidence—that of all the tales in the world I should have been reading the previous evening, that sweetly melancholy one of O'Henry about the people who all unwittingly give presents that can no longer be of any value to their recipients. . . .

"If you should see Alexa," cried Miriam after me, "tell her to let me know at least when she's coming home."

My foot, as I turned, had caught the edge of the package still leaning against the lintel. With a small whispering from its jostled contents it now fell forward into the hallway where Miriam stood, rocking gently for a moment at her feet.

"Alexa," I said, into infinity—"has come home."

THE TOMBLING DAY

Ray Bradbury

IT WAS THE Tombling day, and all the people had walked up the summer road, including Grandma Loblilly, and they stood now in the green day and the high sky country of Missouri, and there was a smell of the seasons changing and the grass breaking out in flowers.

"Here we are," said Grandma Loblilly, over her cane, and she gave them all a flashing look of her yellow-brown eyes and spat into the dust.

The graveyard lay on the side of a quiet hill. It was a place of sunken mounds and wooden markers: bees hummed all about in quietudes of sound, and butterflies withered and blossomed on the clear blue air. The tall sunburned men and ginghamed women stood a long silent time looking in at their deep and buried relatives.

"Well, let's get to work!" said Grandma, and she hobbled across the moist grass, sticking it rapidly, here and there, with her cane.

The others brought the spades and special crates, with daisies and lilacs tied brightly to them. The government was cutting a road through here in August, and since this graveyard had gone unused for fifty years the relatives had agreed to untuck all the old bones and pat them snug somewhere else.

Grandma Loblilly got right down on her knees and trembled a spade in her hand. The others were busy at their own places.

"Grandma," said Joseph Pikes, making a big shadow on her working. "Grandma, you shouldn't be workin' on this place. This's William Simmons' grave, Grandma."

At the sound of his voice, everyone stopped working and listened, and there was just the sound of butterflies on the cool afternoon air.

Grandma looked up at Pikes. "You think I don't *know* it's *his* place? I ain't seen William Simmons in sixty years, but I intend to visit him today." She patted out trowel after trowel of rich soil, and she grew quiet and introspective and said things to the day and those who might listen. "Sixty years ago, and him a fine man, only twenty-three. And me, I was twenty and all golden about the head and all milk in my arms and neck and persimmon in my cheeks. Sixty years and a planned marriage, and then a sickness and him dying away. And me alone, and I remember how the earth-mound over him sank in the rains—"

Everybody stared at Grandma.

"But, still, Grandma—" said Joseph Pikes.

The grave was shallow. She soon reached the long iron box.

"Gimme a hand!" she cried.

Nine men helped lift the iron box out of the earth, Grandma poking at them with her cane. "Careful!" she shouted. "Easy!" she cried. "Now." They set it on the ground. "Now," she said, "if you be so kindly, you gentlemen might fetch Mr. Simmons on up to my house for a spell."

"We're takin' him on to the new cemetery," said Joseph Pikes.

Grandma fixed him with her needle eyes. "You just trot that box right up to my house. Much obliged."

The men watched her dwindle down the road. They looked at the box, looked at each other, and then spat on their hands.

Five minutes later the men squeezed the iron coffin through the front door of Grandma's little white house and set the box down by the potbelly stove.

She gave them a drink all around. "Now, let's lift the lid," she said. "It ain't every day you see old friends."

The men did not move.

"Well, if you won't, I will." She thrust at the lid with her cane, again and again, breaking away the earth crust. Spiders went touching over the floor. There was a rich smell, like plowed spring earth. Now the men fingered the lid. Grandma stood back.

"Up," she said. She gestured her cane, like an ancient goddess. And up in the air went the lid. The men set the case on the floor and turned.

There was a sound like wind sighing in October from all their mouths.

There lay William Simmons as the dust filtered bright and golden through the air. There he slept, a little smile on his lips, hands folded, all dressed up and no place in all the world to go.

Grandma Loblilly gave a low moaning cry.

"He's all there."

There he was, indeed. Intact as a beetle in his shell, his skin all white and fine, his small eyelids over his pretty eyes like flower petals put there, his lips still with color in them, his hair combed neat, his tie tied, his fingernails pared clean. All in all, he was as complete as the day they shoveled the earth upon his silent case.

Grandma stood tightening her eyes, her hands up to catch the breath that moved from her mouth. She couldn't see. "Where's my specs?" she cried. People searched. "Can't you find 'em?" she shouted. She squinted at the body. "Never mind," she said, getting close. The room settled. She sighed and quavered and cooed over the opened box.

"He's kept," said one of the women. "He ain't crumbled."

"Things like that," said Joseph Pikes, "don't happen."

"It *happened,*" said the woman.

"Sixty years underground. Stands to reason no man lasts that long."

The sunlight was late by each window, the last butterflies were settling among flowers to look like nothing more than other flowers.

Grandma Loblilly put out her wrinkly hand, trembling. "The earth kept him. The way the air is. That was good dry soil for keeping."

"He's young." wailed one of the women, quietly. "So young."

"Yes," said Grandma Loblilly, looking at him. "Him, lying there, twenty-three years old. And me, standing here, pushing eighty!" She shut her eyes.

"Now, Grandma." Joseph Pikes touched her shoulder.

"Yes, him lyin' there, all twenty-three and fine and purty, and *me*—" She squeezed her eyes tight. "Me bending over him, never young again myself, only old and spindly, never to have a chance at being young again. Oh, Lord! Death keeps people young. Look how kind death's been to him." She ran her hands over her body and face slowly, turning to the others. "Death's nicer than life. Why didn't I die then, too? Then we'd both be young now, together. Me in my box, in my white wedding gown all lace, and my eyes closed down, all shy with death. And my hands making a prayer on my bosom."

"Grandma, don't carry on."

"I got a *right* to carry on! Why didn't *I* die, too? Then, when he came back, like he came today, to see me, I wouldn't be like *this*!"

Her hands went wildly to feel her lined face, to twist the loose skin, to fumble the empty mouth, to yank the gray hair and look at it with appalled eyes.

"What a fine coming-back he's had!" She showed her skinny arms. "Think that a man of twenty-three years will want the likes of a seventy-nine-year woman with sump-rot in her veins? I been cheated! Death kept him young forever. Look at me: did *Life* do so much?"

"There're compensations," said Joseph Pikes. "He ain't young, Grandma. He's long over eighty years."

"You're a fool, Joseph Pikes. He's fine as a stone, not touched by a thousand rains. And he's come back to see me, and he'll be picking one of the younger girls now. What would he want with an old woman?"

"He's in no way to fetch nuthin' offa nobody," said Joseph Pikes.

Grandma pushed him back. "Get out now, all of you! Ain't *your* box, ain't your lid, and it ain't your almost-husband! You leave the box here, leastwise tonight, and tomorrow you dig a new burying place."

"Awright, Grandma; he was your beau. I'll come early tomorrow. Don't you cry, now."

"I'll do what my eyes most need to do."

She stood stiff in the middle of the room, until the last of them were out the door. After a while she got a candle and lit it, then she noticed someone standing on the hill outside. It was Joseph Pikes. He'd be there the rest of the night, she reckoned, and she did not shout for him to go away. She did not look out the window again, but she knew he was there, and so was much better rested in the following hours.

She went to the coffin and looked down at William Simmons.

She gazed fully upon him. Seeing his hands was like seeing actions. She saw how they had been with the reins of a horse in them, moving up and down. She remembered how the lips of him had clucked as the carriage had glided along with an even pacing of the horse through the meadowlands, the moonlit shadows all around. She knew how it was when those hands held you.

She touched his suit. "That's not the same suit he was buried in!" she cried suddenly. And yet she knew it was the same. Sixty years had changed not the suit but the linings of her mind.

Seized with quick fear, she hunted a long time until she found her spectacles and put them on.

"Why, *that's* not William Simmons!" she shouted.

But she knew this also to be untrue. It *was* William Simmons. "His chin didn't go back *that* far!" she cried softly, logically. "Or *did* it?" And his hair. "It was a wonderful sorrel color, I remember! This hair here's just plain brown. And his nose. I don't recall it being *that* tippy!"

She stood over this strange man and, gradually, as she watched, she knew that this indeed *was* William Simmons. She knew a thing she should have known all along: that dead people are like wax-memory—you take them in your mind, you shape and squeeze and fix them, push a bump here, stretch one out there, pull the body tall, shape and reshape, handle, sculpt, and finish a man-memory until he's all out of kilter.

There was a certain sense of loss and bewilderment in her. She wished she had never opened the box. Or, leastwise, had the sense to leave her glasses off. She had not seen him clearly at first; just enough so she filled in the rough spots with her mind. Now, with her glasses on . . .

She glanced again and again at his face. It became slowly familiar. That memory of him that she had torn apart and put together for sixty years faded, to be replaced by the man she had *really* known. And he was *fine* to look upon. The sense of having lost something vanished. He was the same man, no more, no less. This was always the way when you didn't see people for years and they came back to say howdy-do. For a spell you felt so very uneasy with them. But then, at last, you relaxed.

"Yes, that's you," she laughed. "I see you peeking out from behind all the strangeness. I see you all glinty and sly here and there and about."

She began to cry again. If only she could lie to herself, if only she could say, "Look at him, he don't look the same, he's not the same man I took a fetching on!" then she could feel better. But all the little inside-people sitting around in her head would rock back in their tiny rockers and cackle and say, "You ain't foolin' us none, Grandma."

Yes, how easy to deny it was him. And feel better. But she didn't deny it. She felt the great depressing sadness because here he was, young as creek water, and here she was, old as the sea.

"William Simmons!" she cried. "Don't look at me! I *know* you still love me, so I'll primp myself up!"

She stirred the stove-fire, quickly put irons on to heat, used irons on her hair till it was all gray curls. Baking powder whitened her cheeks. She bit a cherry to color her lips, pinched her cheeks to bring a flush. From a trunk she yanked old materials until she found a faded blue velvet dress, which she put on.

She stared wildly in the mirror at herself.

"No, no." She groaned and shut her eyes. "There's nothing I can do to make me younger'n you, William Simmons! Even if I died *now* it wouldn't cure me of this old thing come on me—this disease of age!"

She had a violent wish to run forever in the woods, fall in a leaf-pile and molder down into smoking ruin with them. She ran across the room, intending never to come back. But as she yanked the door wide, a cold wind exploded over her from outside and she heard a sound that made her hesitate.

The wind rushed about the room, yanked at the coffin and pushed inside it.

William Simmons seemed to stir in his box.

Grandma slammed the door.

She moved slowly back to squint at him.

He was ten years older.

There were wrinkles and lines on his hands and face.

"William Simmons!"

During the next hour, William Simmons' face tolled away the years. His cheeks went in on themselves, like clenching a fist, like withering an apple in a bin. His flesh was made of carved pure white snow, and the cabin heat melted it. It got a charred look. The air made the eyes and mouth pucker. Then, as if struck a hammer-blow, the face shattered in an agony of time. It was forty, then fifty, then sixty years old! It was seventy, eighty, one hundred years! Burning, burning away! There were small whispers and leaf-crackles from its face and its age-burning hands, one hundred ten, one hundred twenty years, line upon etched, greaved line!

Grandma Loblilly stood there all the cold night, aching her bird-bones, watching, cold, over the changing man. She was a witness to all improbabilities. She felt something finally let loose of her heart. She did not feel sad any more. The weight lifted away from her.

She went peacefully to sleep, standing against a chair.

Sunlight came yellow through the woodland, birds and ants and creek waters were moving, each as quiet as the other, going somewhere.

It was morning.

Grandma woke and looked down upon William Simmons.

He was nothing but delicate ivory carvings.

"Ah!" said Grandma, looking and seeing.

Her very breath stirred and stirred his bones until they flaked, like a chrysalis, like a kind of candy all whittling away, burning with an invisible fire. The bones flaked and flew, light as pieces of dust on the sunlight. Each time she shouted, the bones split asunder, there was a dry flaking rustle from the box.

If there was a wind and she opened the door, he'd be blown away on it like so many crackly leaves!

She bent for a long time, looking at the box. Then she gave a knowing cry, a sound of discovery and moved back, putting her hands first to her face and then to her spindly breasts and then traveling all up and down her arms and legs and fumbling at her empty mouth.

Her shout brought Joseph Pikes running.

He pulled up at the door only in time to see Grandma Loblilly dancing and jumping around on her yellow, high-peg shoes in a wild gyration.

She clapped hands, laughed, flung her skirts, ran in a circle, and did a little waltz with herself, tears on her face. And to the sunlight and the flashing image of herself in the wall mirror she cried:

"I'm young! I'm eighty, but I'm younger'n *him*!"

She skipped, she hopped, and she curtsied.

"There are compensations, Joseph Pikes; you was right!" she chortled. "I'm younger'n *all* the dead ones in the whole world!"

And she waltzed so violently the whirl of her dress pulled at the box and whispers of chrysalis leaped on the air to hang golden and powdery amid her shouts.

"Whee-*deee*!" she cried. "Whee-*heee*!"

HEAD MAN

Robert Bloch

CHAPTER ONE

KING OF THE CORPSES

HIS NAME WAS Otto Krantz, and he was the greatest actor in Berlin. And was not Berlin the capital of the entire reasonable world? He appeared before the public every day in the same drama, in the same role. Now, in 1937, it appeared as though the show might run forever, but no one seemed bored by his performance. And Otto Krantz did his best to keep it that way. He was never satisfied, but continued to rehearse and seek improvements in his part.

Take the matter of costume, for example. Krantz always appeared in evening clothes, but of a very simple cut. This sober garb was a surprising contrast, for many of the minor players wore gaudy uniforms or sought attention by wearing outlandish rags. But Krantz, after much study, realized his modest attire brought him more popular approval than the extravagant outfits of the others.

Again, the other actors were given to impassioned gestures as gaudy as their clothing. They shouted at the audience, they ranted, raved, wept, scowled, went into hysterics.

The spectators were never impressed. They much preferred the businesslike approach of Otto Krantz, who said little but acted with the finesse of a master. He never played to the gallery. While on stage he went through the "business" as if the audience didn't exist. For this reason Krantz remained the most popular actor in Berlin, playing over and over again the same role in the same comedy—a role no one seemed to tire of.

The comedy was entitled *The Third Reich.*

The stage was the platform of the public executioner.

Otto Krantz filled the role of official headsman.

Each performance boasted a new supporting cast and a growing audience to cheer the comedy on.

It was always the same. Every morning Krantz made his grand entrance in the bleak courtyard, instructed the new players in a stage whisper, and graciously conducted them to the center of the platform. With becoming modesty, the great actor allowed each a moment alone in the spotlight in which to receive the tribute of the spectators.

After this, the show proceeded swiftly. Capable assistants did the placing and the binding—but it was Otto Krantz who tested the straps, bowed politely to the military escort and then raised the bright, shining blade of the headsman's axe from its place in a block of ice.

Then came the glorious moment of climax, the moment that never failed to move both the minor players and the crowd. And when it was over, Otto Krantz lifted the head from the basket and held it up to his applauding audience with an honest smile of workmanlike pride.

This happened not once, but as often as ten or a dozen times in a single morning. Yet Krantz never faltered, never grew tired, never missed a line or a cue.

A sneering aristocrat of the old school, the sniveling young son of a lower-class family, a withered *hausfrau* or a rosy-cheeked beauty—all received the same efficient courtesy at the hands of the executioner—hands that grew stained and red with the drops that fell as each head was lifted from the basket.

Outside of his public appearances, Krantz led a quiet life. A glass of schnapps when work was through, perhaps a little beer to wash down dinner at some humble bierstube, a stroll through the street to hear the news, and then home to the big upstairs room near SS District Headquarters. In the evening there might be a party meeting to attend, or a summons from the Gestapo notifying him of tomorrow's labors.

It was a simple existence, for Otto Krantz did not share the hysteria of the times. He served the Reich with no thought of personal pleasure or profit. Let others raise the rabble and bluster in public meetings. In his time Krantz had cut short a good many of these speakers—cut them short by a neck. These days might bring honors to a wiser head—but many wiser heads fell into his basket.

Krantz was content. A year before, he had been a humble butcher. Since leaving the slaughterhouse for a public post, he had seen enough of the world and its ways, and had met many people. Officially, in the past year, he had met several thousand. Each acquaintance was of painfully short duration, but it was enough.

He had gazed into the faces of the best families of Germany. He had held those faces in his hands—those proud, proud faces that would never smile again. And he knew that the blue bloods stained his axe with gore as red as that of the lowest thief.

So Krantz was content. Until, gradually, the faces came *too fast*. It was impossible to ignore them any longer. He felt himself becoming interested in them because they passed in such an endless variety before his eyes. For each face masked a secret, each skull held a story. Young, old, pure, debauched, innocent, guilty, foolish, wise, shamed, defiant, cringing, bold—ten a day, twenty a day, they mounted the platform and bent their necks to the yoke of death.

Who were these people he conducted into eternity? He, a

simple butcher, was shaping the destiny of Germany. Shaping it with an axe.

What was the nature of that destiny?

These faces knew.

Krantz tried to find out. He began to peer more closely at each prisoner in turn. Without realizing it, he gazed deeper into dead eyes, felt the shapes of skulls, traced the texture of hair and skin.

One day after work he entered a bookstall and bought texts on phrenology and physiography. That had been two months ago, and now he had gone further in his speculations.

Now, when work was through, he went home quickly and threw himself down on the bed. With eyes closed he waited for the facts of the day to pass in review.

They came—pallid faces molded in sadness or rage; three thousand death masks, and the end not yet! And with them came a message.

"You, Otto Krantz, are our master! You are the most powerful man in the Reich. Not Hitler, not Goebbels, not Himmler or the others. You, Otto Krantz, hold the real power of life and death!"

At first, Krantz was afraid of such thoughts. But every day came a dozen new reminders, a dozen new faces to review in darkness, to remember, to relish.

For weeks now his memories had seemed to center around one particular moment—the moment when he held up the head and gazed into the face. Lately he had been forced to hold himself sternly in check as he did so, lest he betray his excitement. This was the supreme thrill, to hold the heads. If there were only some way to recapture that thrill, that sensation of power, at will! If only he could . . .

Steal the heads.

No. That was madness. If he were discovered, he would die. And for what? The foolish face of a gaping old wastrel?

Not that. Not a gray old head with a cruel, stupid face. It was not worth the risk. But there were other heads—strange heads of debauchees, golden heads of beautiful ladies that hung before him in dreams. These were worth possessing.

He must find a way, Krantz decided. It would be necessary to visit the condemned cells nightly, when the lists of execution were given out. Then he could inspect the crop and make his choices. He might make an arrangement with old Fritz, the scavenger who did the burials of all the unclaimed bodies. For a few marks, Fritz would do anything. Then Otto Krantz could go home with a burlap bag slung over his shoulder. Nobody would be the wiser.

Krantz thought it all out carefully. He had to be careful, make sure no one suspected, for if they knew they would not understand. They might think he was crazy and shut him away. Then he wouldn't have his axe any more. He wouldn't be able to polish the heavy, gleaming blade every morning before work started. And he wouldn't see the heads every day. That must not be permitted to happen.

So he was very careful the next few times he went to work. Nobody who noticed the tall, broad-shouldered man with the close-cropped moustache and bald head would suspect that behind his stern, impassive countenance there lurked a dream.

Even his victims didn't realize it when he stared at their faces each morning. Perhaps the black mask he wore helped to disguise the hideous intensity of his searching stare. It also concealed his disappointment.

For none of these traitors had the face that would satisfy him. None seemed to hold the symbol of power he desired. There was nothing but a succession of commonplace countenances. Krantz was disappointed, but he didn't give up.

He went to Gestapo headquarters one evening late in the week. He passed up the broad stairs and received the salute of the troopers with the dignity befitting an official of the Reich. He had no trouble in the outer office.

The man at the desk chuckled when he heard Krantz make his apologetic, humble request.

"You want to see the list for tomorrow? Here, it's ready. Only seven of the swine for high treason. You can probably do the job with one hand."

Otto Krantz didn't laugh. He spoke again, smoothly. "If you please, I should like to see the prisoners."

"*See* them?"

"Yes."

The man at the desk shrugged. "That is very irregular. I'm afraid you'd have to ask Inspector Grunert for permission."

"But can't you—?"

"One must obey orders, you know. Let me announce you." The desk official buzzed the intercom, spoke briefly and then raised his head. "You may go right in," he said, nodding toward the door behind him.

Krantz forced a rigid smile. He had to go through with this, carry it off. If only he could get permission, it would be easy to make further plans.

As he entered Inspector Grunert's office, the rigid smile became suffused with incredulous delight. For there, sitting on the bench before the inspector's desk, were the two prisoners he wanted—the answers to all of his prayers, his dreams.

CHAPTER TWO

THE BLOODY AXE

OTTO KRANTZ stared at them closely, noting with growing pleasure each detail of their faces.

The man was old, with long white hair, but his features were young, smooth, delicately pointed features, lit up by great, green, glowing eyes.

Who was this white-haired ancient with the face of a boy and the eyes and mouth of an unearthly being?

"He is the man I want," whispered the voice within Otto Krantz.

Then he looked at the other prisoner, the woman.

She was beautiful, with titian hair that flowed like flame to her shoulders. Her face was pale, marked by suffering. And she, also, had great, glowing, green eyes.

"She is the woman I want," said the voice within Otto Krantz.

He couldn't tear his eyes from them. The long white hair, the long red hair. The slim necks. The greenish glow of their eyes. Father and daughter? Creatures of another world, a world of dreams. These were the two he wanted. . . .

"Ah, Krantz, here you are." Smiling, Grunert rose and extended a fleshy palm. "Just in time to meet two future clients." The fat inspector bowed sardonically in the direction of the prisoners. "Allow me to present Joachim Fulger and his daughter, Eva."

They did not stir. Neither man nor girl looked at Otto Krantz. Their eyes rejected the presence of the headsman, the inspector, the room itself.

Grunert chuckled. "One runs across all types in the line of duty. Queer fish. Take these two specimens, for example."

"I'm going to," whispered the inner voice.

Grunert could not hear it as he went on. "What do you suppose these two have been doing?" he inquired. "You'll never guess, so I'll tell you. They just signed a confession, in case you don't believe me."

"What?" asked Otto Krantz, knowing it was expected of him.

"Practicing sorcery against the Reich—can you imagine such a thing in this day and age? Sticking pins in images of our Fuehrer!"

Grunert scowled, reflectively. "Their block leader got wind of it last month. Sounded fantastic, but he checked them just as a matter of routine. Everyone in the neighborhood seemed to know they were queer ones—selling love philters, telling fortunes, and all that.

"But when the block leader dropped in to pay them a visit—all very pleasant, not in an official capacity or anything—this swine of a magician and his unnatural offspring put an ice pick into his throat!"

The two prisoners did not stir. Inspector Grunert nodded at Krantz and tapped his head significantly. "You see how it is." He shrugged. "They could get the camp or a firing squad. But I decided the sorcery charge was the one to press. Make it high treason, I said. Herr Goebbels is always looking for a story—and here is a good example to set before those who work secretly against the Fuehrer."

He rose and confronted the silent, unblinking pair. "Cool as cucumbers, aren't they? But they cursed enough when we had them brought in, I can tell you! A few days here and they signed the confession without a murmur.

"Maybe they're wise at that. This old bag of bones wouldn't dance very long at the end of a whip, I don't suppose. And as for the girl, it would be a shame to mar such beauty. A pity she's a witch."

Grunert brushed one hand through her flaming hair, then drew it away as if the hair were indeed aflame. He stepped back hastily.

"There *is* something odd about this pair of fools, at that," he muttered. "Crazy fanatics! Trying to kill men by sticking pins in photographs and dolls. Why, it's barbaric!"

A laugh crawled up out of Joachim Fulger's white throat. The voice that followed it was curiously disturbing.

"Do you hear, Eva, my child? *We* are barbaric, says this barbarian in his murderer's uniform! He sits here in his torture chamber and explains our barbarism to the brutal savage whose axe will shear our heads from our necks tomorrow morning."

Again, the laughter.

The girl's voice came now. Soft, vibrant, intense. "We are sorcerers, by his standards. But our magic is cleaner than the black and evil spells of these madmen with their chanting slogans, their howling worship of ancient gods. Our crime is that we have fought evil, and apparently we have lost.

"But the day will come. Those who take the sword must perish by the sword; those who take whips shall die beneath them, and those who wield the axe will lie beneath it."

The words moved Krantz, until he remembered she was possessed—a witch, a lunatic. But she was beautiful.

"Let them rave," Grunert chuckled. "But you wanted to see me about something, Krantz?"

"It does not matter. Some other time," muttered the headsman. "I will go now."

"Very well." Grunert faced the prisoners. "You will meet Krantz again tomorrow morning. Perhaps then he can match your sharp tongues with something sharper. Eh, Otto?"

"Yes," Krantz whispered. Then, abruptly, he turned and stumbled out of the room. He had remembered a duty to perform. A most important duty. He had to get back to his room and begin.

It wasn't until he busied himself at the vital task that Krantz permitted himself to feel the thrill of anticipation again. But then it could no longer be held back, and Otto Krantz grinned in glee as he sat in the darkness of his room and delicately sharpened his axe.

"You want I should let you have the heads from those two bodies and bury the corpses secretly? *Nein!*" Fritz the scavenger shook his tousled gray head in bewildered but emphatic denial.

"But nobody has registered to claim the bodies. No one will know if you quicklime them *with* the heads or not," Krantz wheedled.

"I cannot do this thing," Fritz grumbled.

Otto Krantz smiled. He had anticipated some little show of resistance by the scavenger. He now anticipated the melting of that resistance when he offered his bribe.

"Fifty marks in it for you," he whispered.

Fritz blinked. But still he shook his head.

"I can get you extra butter rations," Krantz murmured. "I will talk to the district leader tomorrow."

Fritz sighed. "I would do it for you without pay," he said. "But I cannot. You see, the Fulgers are not going to be beheaded, after all."

Then and only then did Otto Krantz realize how much the possession of those two heads meant to him.

He had come away from his room in the middle of the night, carrying his axe in its velvet case. He had scurried through the streets, his official evening dress gaining him free passage from any SS troopers encountered on the way. He had hurried here to the little room beneath the cell blocks where Fritz the scavenger lived. And all the while he had been hugging the thought of what was to come, gloating over the attainment of his goal.

Now the opportunity had slipped away.

With it, something slipped in Otto Krantz's brain. He could feel it, the usurpation of his consciousness by that single pulsing urge. He couldn't define the sensation. He knew only one thing—he must get those heads.

Krantz thought fast, spoke rapidly. "Fritz!"

"Yes?"

"Is it still true that no one has claimed the bodies?"

"Yes, that is so."

"Then after the Fulgers are shot, you will still take them to the lime vats?"

"I suppose."

"Who has signed the papers for execution?"

"No one, of course. You remember, Inspector Grunert always does that when he arrives, first thing in the morning."

Krantz rubbed his hands. "So no orders have actually been issued yet. No firing squad is appointed, no time has been set?"

"That is true."

"Very well, then. Fritz, I offer a hundred marks to you for the heads."

"But there will be no heads, I tell you. They'll be shot."

Krantz smiled. "No, they won't! I'm taking the Fulgers out to the yard right now. I'll get the job over with before the official ceremony begins at dawn."

"But the orders—"

"Who will know? I'll tell Grunert I picked up the order along with the rest at his office and took the liberty of assigning a squad to do the job, just to save him the trouble. He'll sign the order afterward and forget about it. He'll never bother to ask who did the shooting, and since the bodies are unclaimed, you can cart them away."

"The risk, they'll see you do it. . . ."

"No one will see. I shall bring them here myself."

"Here, to my room?"

"I'll tidy it up again for you, my fastidious friend."

"No. I won't permit it. We'll be caught."

"Fritz."

Krantz's voice was very soft as he uttered the name. But his face was hard. His hands, his butcher's hands, were harder as they closed about the throat of the old scavenger.

"You will do what I command, Fritz," he whispered. He squeezed, for emphasis. Not too hard, but enough to convince.

Fritz fell back, choking, and clawed impotently at his tortured throat. "Yes—yes—but hurry! It's nearly dawn now."

Krantz hurried.

He picked up the necessary papers in the inspector's office. He raced down the silent, night-lighted halls to the cell blocks, located a blinking guard and bawled orders to the surprised fellow in convincing tones.

"Where's the escort?" the guard protested.

"Upstairs, waiting," snapped Krantz.

"You're going to take them up alone?"

"You saw the orders. Get the Fulgers for me. At once, *Dummkopf!*"

Befuddled, the guard led him to the cell.

"Raus!"

The Fulgers were waiting, their green eyes gleaming in the murky dawn.

There was no trouble. They preceded Krantz up the stairs without a word. The headsman followed, slamming the outer door in the guard's face.

"This way," said Otto Krantz. He indicated a door.

Fulger and his daughter obeyed. The outer halls were deserted, and Krantz, with a pounding heart, knew that they would reach Fritz's quarters without being seen.

They did.

Fritz had everything in readiness. He'd hauled out an extra block of ice, and the axe was imbedded deeply therein, to keep the edge sharp. He had set up the official block as well. The basket and sawdust were waiting. It was all done in the proper regulation manner, just as it would be outside. He handed Otto Krantz the headsman's mask.

Krantz donned it.

Joachim and Eva Fulger stood against the wall of the little room under the cell blocks and stared. The old man turned to Krantz.

"But the court decreed that we be shot," he murmured. "Why the axe? And why here, inside? Where are the guards, where are the officials?"

The bony fingers of Otto Krantz raked across his mouth. "Silence!"

Eva's expression did not change. She merely opened her mouth a trifle and screamed.

Krantz stopped that. Her curls helped. Twisted expertly about her throat, they muffled further outcry.

Fritz had the old man kneeling now. He kicked the block into place.

Krantz drew the axe from the ice.

There was a deathly silence in the little room.

Joachim Fulger's words came very faintly, but quite clearly. "So. This is the end. But not the end."

Krantz grunted. The blade was heavy.

"I warn you," murmured Joachim Fulger. "As ye sow, so shall ye reap."

Krantz had a sharp retort for that—the axe.

CHAPTER THREE

NIGHTMARE

THE NIGHTMARE was over. Cleaning the room, hiding the bodies until they were ready for the lime, getting the burlap sack—Fritz attended to all that.

Otto Krantz appeared in the courtyard promptly at dawn, ready for his official duties. Grunert was there, and some others. The victims were led out. Krantz labored.

It was all a red blur. He plodded through his task mechanically now, as he had in the slaughterhouse long ago. The significance was gone from the moment. Sheep bleated, sheep died.

He could hardly wait to get home. . . .

Grunert casually inquired about the Fulgers, after the executions were over. Krantz mentioned taking the liberty of arranging for the firing squad on his own authority, then quite indifferently presented the order for signing. Grunert shrugged, signed without reading, and sent it along with the rest for the official files.

It was over, and Otto Krantz had his sack. He hugged it to his breast as he sped through the streets toward home. He ran the last few blocks, his feet moving in rhythm with his pulsing heart.

When he locked himself in the room, he was trembling with anticipation.

White-haired Joachim and auburn-tressed Eva stared up at him with glowing eyes. Their faces were set in grimaces of undying hate.

Someone seeing him right now might think him mad, Krantz

reflected. But he was not mad. No madman would be as clever, as cunning, as crafty as he.

These two had been mad. Mad, with their babbling of sorcery and witchcraft. They had not even had the sense to be afraid of death. They had mocked him, ridiculed him, called him a crude barbarian.

Well, perhaps he was a barbarian. A headhunter, maybe. Like those Indians in South America—Jivaros, weren't they? That was what he was, a headhunter!

It was quite a joke, Krantz laughed.

They had mocked him, these two, so now he mocked them. He talked to the heads for a long time. He flung their words in their teeth. "Those that live by the axe shall perish beneath it," they had said. And, "As ye sow, so shall ye reap."

Krantz told them what he thought of that. He told them a great deal. After a while he no longer realized that he was talking to the dead. The heads seemed to nod and shake in answer to his words. The grins expanded sardonically.

They were laughing at him!

Krantz grew angry. He shouted at the heads. He shouted so loudly that at first he didn't hear the knocking on his door.

Then, when it rose to thunderous crescendo, he turned.

With a start he realized it was already dusk. Where had the day gone to?

The knocking persisted.

Krantz got out the burlap bag, filled it and shoved it under his bed. Then he answered the door, straightening his collar and striving to control the trembling of his lips.

"*Lieber Gott,* let me in!"

It was Fritz, the scavenger. He stood quivering in the doorway until Otto Krantz dragged him across the threshold by the scruff of the neck.

"What is it, you fool?"

"We are undone, Herr Krantz."

"Speak up, you fool! Here, sit down and tell me, but be quick about it."

"The Fulgers—their bodies have been claimed by a relative. A cousin, I think. He comes tonight to take them for burial."

"No, he can't do that!"

"But he is, he has received permission. And we shall be found out, and it will mean the axe for us."

"Wait a minute."

Krantz managed to control his voice. He thought fast, frantically. Desperation blossomed into inspiration.

"Where are the bodies now?" he whispered.

"I have them out at the lime pits, behind the walls—near the old quarry."

"No one has seen them?"

"Not yet." Fritz gulped anxiously.

"And this cousin of the Fulgers will not come for them until late tonight?"

"That is right. He has received permission to bring a hearse and two coffins."

"Burial at once, I presume?"

"That is the law. You know it."

Otto Krantz smiled. "Good. We shall be all right, then. I have thought of a way." He patted Fritz on the shoulder. "This cousin of the Fulgers will not examine the bodies too closely, I think. He will not even bother to search for bullet wounds."

"But they are headless."

"Exactly." A smile crept over Krantz's face. Even in the twilight Fritz could see that smile, and he shuddered.

"What will you do?" he croaked.

"Do you remember the last words of Joachim Fulger?" Krantz whispered.

"Yes. As ye sow, so shall ye reap. That's from the Bible, isn't it?"

"Exactly," Krantz grinned. "The old fool meant it as a warning. Instead, it will be our salvation."

"But I don't see—"

"Never mind. Do as you're ordered, if you want to save your scrawny neck. Go at once to the shop down the street. Purchase five yards of strong catgut and a surgical needle. I will meet you at the lime pits tonight at eight. I'll bring the sack with me. Now do you understand?"

Fritz understood. He was still shuddering as Krantz pushed him out into the hall toward the stairs.

It was a grisly ordeal. They worked in darkness, lest a light betray their presence to SS troopers on guard in the pits beyond.

They crouched in the little shed in utter blackness and groped their way about the business in silence. Fortunately there was no trouble in locating the bodies. Fritz had carefully set them aside for immediate interment.

The rest was up to Krantz. He was no surgeon, but his fingers held a skill born of utter desperation. If he bungled the task, his life was forfeit, and he knew it. He strung the catgut and sewed.

The needle rose and fell, rose and fell, rose and fell in darkness as Otto Krantz pursued his ghastly fancywork.

And then it was done—done amid the shuddering whimpers that rose from Fritz's frantic throat.

But Krantz held his nerve to the last. It was he who added the final touch—binding the high collars about the two white throats. At last he sighed, signifying that the task was complete.

Fritz wanted to bolt for it then. Krantz whispered that he must wait, must hide by the wall across the way from the shed, until they saw the cousin actually come and take the bodies away. Then and only then would he be certain of their safety.

So they waited, waited until midnight in the darkness. What phantasms it held for Fritz, Otto Krantz could not say. But as he stared into the night he saw the grinning faces of Joachim and Eva Fulger hanging bodiless in midair, their eyes alive with undying mockery.

Krantz pressed his eyelids together, but the faces remained, their leering mouths twisted as though in an effort to speak from beyond the barrier of death.

What were they trying to tell him?

Krantz didn't know. He didn't want to know. The hands that had wielded the surgical needle so expertly now hung limply at his sides as he waited.

Then the hearse came. The cousin, escorted by a guard, went into the little shed. Two mortician's assistants brought the coffins. Krantz held his breath as they disappeared inside the shed.

They were not inside long. Soon they reappeared, carrying the closed coffins. They did not speak; there was no sign of agitation. The coffins were placed inside the hearse and the car drove away.

It was then that Krantz broke and ran, sobbing, from the scene.

He was safe. Everything was over, and he was safe. The heads were back on their bodies.

He got to his room somehow. Perhaps he might snatch a few hours of sleep before dawn. Then he must get up and return to duty as though nothing had happened.

But Otto Krantz did not sleep.

The heads were back on their bodies, yet they would not go away. They were waiting for Krantz in his room. He saw them hanging in the shadows, even when he turned on the lights.

They hung there—the head of the old man with the long white hair, and the head of the girl with her flaming curls—and they laughed at Krantz.

Let them laugh! He was Otto Krantz, Headsman of the Reich, whom all men feared.

Let them grin their idiotic grins. He had outsmarted them, after all. Now they would be buried away in a grave, and no one would ever know that Krantz had murdered them.

He almost welcomed the coming of dawn in this changed mood. He donned his immaculate evening dress carefully. He brushed his stiff collar into place before the bureau. The heads laughed at him over his shoulder in the mirror, but he didn't care about that now.

He swaggered through the street on his way to headquarters, cradling the axe in its case against his brawny chest. A passing guard drew stiffly to attention as Krantz marched by, then shrank back in sudden fear as he recognized the executioner of the Reich.

Otto Krantz knew he had nothing to fear. He would go about his duties today without question. He squared his shoulders and marched up the steps, into the outer office. He wasn't worried. He knew no one else could see the heads but he himself.

He smiled at the man behind the desk. That was the way—brazen it out!

"I'd like to see Inspector Grunert, please. About today's orders. Is he here yet?"

The inspector left word for you to go right in."

There. The inspector was waiting for him. That was the kind of a man Otto Krantz was. Inspectors waited for his arrival.

He strutted into Inspector Grunert's office.

The inspector *was* waiting.

Krantz realized that just as soon as the two Gestapo men stepped from behind the door and pinned his arms close to his sides.

"Otto Krantz, I arrest you in the name of the Third Reich, for the murder of Joachim and Eva Fulger."

But what was he talking about? The Fulgers were in their graves by now, buried.

No—they weren't.

The inspector was pulling the sheet from the table over in the corner.

Otto Krantz stared. He saw the heads again, and this time everyone could see them. They were grinning up at him now from over the tops of the sheets.

They looked all right. The heads had been sewn on tightly. Perfectly. The high collars were still in place. Nothing was wrong with his work, nothing looked suspicious. Why, the collars hadn't even been pulled back to disclose his sewing!

Then what was wrong?

Krantz gazed at the still bodies, trying to read the secret. He didn't hear any of Inspector Grunert's mumblings about madmen, about murder. He was trying to remember what had happened.

"As ye sow," the old man had warned. *"As ye sow . . ."*

Then Otto Krantz's gaze traveled up again to the heads of the dead wizard and his daughter. He screamed, once.

"Too bad you didn't have any light to work with in that shed," Inspector Grunert purred.

Otto Krantz didn't hear him.

He was staring at the grinning heads of the old man and the girl—the heads he had sewed back on in the darkness and had inadvertently switched.

THE DEMON LOVER

Elizabeth Bowen

Toward the end of the day in London, Mrs. Drover went around to her shut-up house to look for several things she wanted to take away. Some belonged to her, some to her family, who were by now used to their country life. It was late August; it had been a steamy, showery day; at the moment the trees down the pavement glittered in an escape of humid yellow afternoon sun. Against the next batch of clouds, already piling up ink-dark, broken chimneys and parapets stood out. In her once-familiar street, as in any unused channel, an unfamiliar queerness had silted up; a cat wove itself in and out of railings, but no human eye watched Mrs. Drover's return. Shifting some parcels under her arm, she slowly forced around her latchkey in an unwilling lock, then gave the door, which had warped, a push with her knee. Dead air came out to meet her as she went in.

The staircase window having been boarded up, no light came down into the hall. But one door, she could just see, stood ajar, so she went quickly through into the room and unshuttered the big window in there. Now the prosaic woman, looking about her, was more perplexed than she knew by everything she saw, by traces of her long former habit of life—the yellow smoke stain up the white marble mantelpiece, the ring left by a vase on the top of the escritoire; the bruise in the wallpaper where, on the door being thrown open widely, the china handle had always hit the wall. The piano, having gone away to be stored, had left what looked like claw-marks on its part of the parquet. Though not much dust had seeped in, each object wore a film of another kind; and, the only ventilation being the chimney, the whole drawing room smelled of the cold hearth. Mrs. Drover put down her parcels on the escritoire and left the room to proceed upstairs; the things she wanted were in a bedroom chest.

She had been anxious to see how the house was—the part-time caretaker she shared with some neighbors was away this week on his holiday, known to be not yet back. At the best of times he did not look in often, and she was never sure that she trusted him. There were some cracks in the structure, left by the last bombing, on which she was anxious to keep an eye. Not that one could do anything—

A shaft of refracted daylight now lay across the hall. She stopped dead and stared at the hall table—on this lay a letter addressed to her.

She thought first—then the caretaker *must* be back. All the same, who, seeing the house was shuttered, would have dropped a letter in at the box? It was not a circular, it was not a bill. And the post office redirected, to the address in the country, everything for her that came through the post. The caretaker (even if he *was* back) did not know she was due in London today—her call here had been planned to be a surprise—so his negligence in the manner of this letter, leaving it to wait in the dusk and the dust, annoyed her. Annoyed, she picked up the letter, which bore no stamp. But it cannot be important, or they would know. . . . She took the letter rapidly upstairs with her, without a stop to look at the writing till she reached what had been her bedroom, where she let in light. The room looked over the garden and other gardens: the sun had gone in; as the clouds sharpened and lowered, the trees and rank lawns seemed already to smoke with dark. Her reluctance to look again at the letter came from the fact that she felt intruded upon—and by someone contemptuous of her ways. However, in the tenseness preceding the fall of rain she read it: it was a few lines.

Dear Kathleen,

You will not have forgotten that today is our anniversary, and the day we said. The years have gone by at once slowly and fast. In view of the fact that nothing has changed, I shall rely upon you to keep your promise. I was sorry to see you leave London, but was satisfied that you would be back in time. You may expect me, therefore, at the hour arranged.

Until then . . .

K

Mrs. Drover looked for the date: it was today's. She dropped the letter onto the bedsprings, then picked it up to see the writing again—her lips, beneath the remains of lipstick, beginning to go white. She felt so much the change in her own face that she went to the mirror, polishing a clear patch in it and looked at once urgently and stealthily in. She was confronted by a woman of forty-four, with eyes starting out under a hat-brim that had been rather carelessly pulled down. She had not put on any more powder since she left the shop where she ate her solitary tea. The pearls her husband had given her on their marriage hung loose around her now rather thinner throat, slipping into the V of the pink wool jumper her sister knitted last autumn as they sat around the fire. Mrs. Drover's most normal expression was one of controlled worry, but of assent. Since the birth of the third of her little boys, attended by a quite serious illness, she had had an intermittent muscular flicker to the left of her mouth, but in spite of this she could always sustain a manner that was at once energetic and calm.

Turning from her own face as precipitately as she had gone to meet it, she went to the chest where the things were, unlocked it, threw up the lid and knelt to search. But as rain began to come crashing down she could not keep from looking over her shoulder at the stripped bed on which the letter lay. Behind the blanket of rain, the clock of the church that still stood struck six—with rapidly heightening apprehension she counted each of the slow strokes. "The hour arranged . . . My God," she said, "*what* hour? How should I . . . ? After twenty-five years. . . ."

The young girl talking to the soldier in the garden had not ever completely seen his face. It was dark; they were saying good-bye under a tree. Now and then—for it felt, from not seeing him at this intense moment, as though she had never seen him at all—she verified his presence for these few moments longer by putting out a hand, which he each time pressed, without very much kindness, and painfully, onto one of the breast buttons of his uniform. That cut of the button on the palm of her hand was, principally, what she was to carry away. This was so near the end of a leave from France that she could only wish him already gone. It was August 1916. Being not kissed, being drawn away from and looked at intimidated Kathleen till she imagined spectral glitters in the place of his eyes. Turning away and looking back up the lawn she saw, through branches of trees, the drawing-room window alight; she caught a breath for the moment when she could go running back there into the safe arms of her mother and sister, and cry: "What shall I do, what shall I do? He has gone."

Hearing her catch her breath, her fiancé said, without feeling: "Cold?"

"You're going away such a long way."

"Not so far as you think."

"I don't understand."

"You don't have to," he said. "You will. You know what we said."

"But that was—suppose you—I mean, suppose."

"I shall be with you," he said, "sooner or later. You won't forget that. You need do nothing but wait."

Only a little more than a minute later she was free to run up the silent lawn. Looking in through the window at her mother and sister, who did not for the moment perceive her, she already felt that unnatural promise drive down between her and the rest of all humankind. No other way of having given herself could have made her feel so apart, lost and forsworn. She could not have plighted a more sinister troth.

Kathleen behaved well when, some months later, her fiancé was reported missing, presumably killed. Her family not only supported her but were able to praise her courage without stint because they could not regret, as a husband for her, the man they knew nothing about. They hoped she would, in a year or two, console herself—and had it been only a question of consolation, things might have gone much straighter ahead. But her trouble, beyond just a little grief, was a complete dislocation from everything. She did not reject other lovers, for these failed to appear: for years she failed to attract men—and with the approach of her thirties she became natural enough to share her family's anxiousness on this score. She began to put herself out, to wonder, and at thirty-two she was very greatly relieved to find herself being courted by William Drover. She married him, and the two of them settled down in this quiet, arboreal part of Kensington; in this house the years piled up, her children were born, and they all lived till they were driven out by the bombs of the next war. Her movements as Mrs. Drover were circumscribed, and she dismissed any idea that they were still watched.

As things were—dead or living, the letter writer sent her only a threat. Unable, for some minutes, to go on kneeling with her back exposed to the empty room, Mrs. Drover rose from the chest to sit on an upright chair whose back was firmly against the wall. The desuetude of her former bedroom, her married London home's whole air of being a cracked cup from which memory, with its reassuring power, had either evaporated or leaked away, made a crisis—and at just this crisis the letter writer had, knowledgeably, struck. The hollowness of the house this evening canceled years on years of voices, habits and steps. Through the shut windows she only heard rain fall on the roofs around. To rally herself, she said she was in a mood—and, for two or three seconds shutting her eyes, told herself that she had imagined the letter. But she opened them—there it lay on the bed.

On the supernatural side of the letter's entrance she was not permitting her mind to dwell. Who, in London, knew she meant to call at the house today? Evidently, however, this had to be known. The caretaker, *had* he come back, had had no cause to expect her: he would have taken the letter in his pocket to forward it, in his own time, through the post. There was no other sign that the caretaker had been in—but, if not? Letters dropped in at doors of deserted houses do not fly or walk to tables in halls. They do not sit on the dust of empty tables with the air of certainty that they will be found. There is needed some human hand—but nobody but the caretaker had a key. Under circumstances she did not care to consider, a house can be entered without a key. It was possible that she was not alone now. She might be being waited for, downstairs. Waited for—until when? Until "the hour arranged." At least that was not six o'clock; six had struck.

She rose from the chair and went over and locked the door.

The thing was to get out. To fly? No, not that: she had to catch her train. As a woman whose utter dependability was the keystone of her family life, she was not willing to return to the country, to her husband, her little boys and her sister without the objects she had come up to fetch. Resuming work at the chest, she set about making up a number of parcels in a rapid, fumbling-decisive way. These were her shopping parcels, would be too much to carry; these meant a taxi—at the thought of the taxi her heart went up and her normal breathing resumed. I will ring up the taxi now; the taxi cannot come too soon; I shall hear the taxi out there running its engine, till I walk calmly down to it through the hall. I'll ring up— But no; the telephone is cut off. . . . She tugged at a knot she had tied wrong.

The idea of flight . . . He was never kind to me, not really. I don't remember him kind at all. Mother said he never considered me. He was set on me, *that* was what it was—not love. Not love, not meaning a person well. What did he do, to make me promise like that? I can't remember—but she found that she could.

She remembered with such dreadful acuteness that the twenty-five years since then dissolved like smoke and she instinctively looked for the weal left by the button on the palm of her hand. She remembered not only all that he said and did but the complete suspension of *her* existence during that August week. I was not myself—they all told me so at the time. She remembered—but with one white burning blank as where acid has dropped on a photograph; *under no conditions* could she remember his face.

So, wherever he may be waiting, I shall not know him. You have no time to run from a face you do not expect.

The thing was to get to the taxi before any clock struck what could be the hour. She would slip down the street and around the side of the square to where the square gave on the main road. She would return in the taxi, safe, to her own door, and bring the solid driver into the house with her to pick up the parcels from room to room. The idea of the taxi driver made her decisive, bold; she unlocked her door, went to the top of the staircase, and listened down.

She heard nothing—but while she was hearing nothing the passé air of the staircase was disturbed by a draft that traveled up to her face. It emanated from the basement; down there a door or window was being opened by someone who chose this moment to leave the house.

The rain had stopped; the pavements steamily shone as Mrs. Drover let herself out by inches from her own front door into the empty street. The unoccupied houses opposite continued to meet her look with their damaged stare. Making toward the thoroughfare and the taxi, she tried not to keep looking behind. Indeed, the silence was so intense—one of those creeks of London silence exaggerated this summer by the damage of war—that no tread could have gained on hers unheard. Where her street debouched on the square where people went on living, she grew conscious of and checked her unnatural pace. Across the open end of the square two buses impassively passed each other; women, a perambulator, cyclists, a man wheeling a barrow signaled, once again, the ordinary flow of life. At the square's most populous corner should be—and was—the short taxi rank. This evening, only one taxi—but this, although it presented its blank rump, appeared already to be alertly waiting for her. Indeed, without looking around, the drive started his engine as she panted up from behind and put her hand on the door. As she did so, the clock struck seven. The taxi faced the main road; to make the trip back to her house, it would have to turn—she had settled back on the seat and the taxi *had* turned before she, surprised by its knowing movement, recollected that she had not "said where." She leaned forward to tap on the glass panel that divided the driver's head from her own.

The driver braked to what was almost a stop, turned around and slid the glass panel back; the jolt of this flung Mrs. Drover forward till her face was almost into the glass. Through the aperture, driver and passenger, not six inches between them, remained for an eternity eye to eye. Mrs. Drover's mouth hung open for some seconds before she could issue her first scream. After that she continued to scream freely and to beat with her gloved hands on the glass all around as the taxi, accelerating without mercy, made off with her into the hinterland of deserted streets.

THE SHUTTERED ROOM

H. P. Lovecraft

I

At dusk, the wild, lonely country guarding the approaches to the village of Dunwich in north-central Massachusetts seems more desolate and forbidding than it ever does by day. Twilight lends the barren fields and domed hills a strangeness that sets them apart from the country around that area; it brings to everything a kind of sentient, watchful animosity—to the ancient trees, to the brier-bordered stone walls pressing close upon the dusty road, to the low marshes with their myriads of fireflies and their incessantly calling whippoorwills vying with the muttering of frogs and the shrill songs of toads, to the sinuous windings of the upper reaches of the Miskatonic flowing among the dark hills seaward, all of which seem to close in upon the traveler as if intent upon holding him fast, beyond all escape.

On his way to Dunwich, Abner Whateley felt all this again, as once in childhood he had felt it and run screaming in terror to beg his mother to take him away from Dunwich and Grandfather Luther Whateley. So many years ago! He had lost count of them. It was curious that the country should affect him so, pushing through all the years he had lived since then—the years at the Sorbonne, in Cairo, in London—pushing through all the learning he had assimilated since those early visits to grim old Grandfather Whateley in his ancient house attached to the mill along the Miskatonic, the country of his childhood, coming back now out of the mists of time as were it but yesterday that he had visited his kinfolk.

They were all gone now—Mother, Grandfather Whateley, Aunt Sarey, whom he had never seen but only knew to be living somewhere in that old house—the loathsome Cousin Wilbur and his terrible twin brother few had ever known before his frightful death on top of Sentinel Hill. But Dunwich, he saw as he drove through the cavernous covered bridge, had not changed; its main street lay under the looming mound of Round Mountain, its gambrel roofs as rotting as ever, its houses deserted, the only store still in the broken-steepled church, over everything the unmistakable aura of decay.

He turned off the main street and followed a rutted road up along the river, until he came within sight of the great old house with the mill wheel on the riverside. It was his property now, by the will of Grandfather Whateley, who had stipulated that he must settle the estate and take such steps as may be necessary to bring about "that dissolution I myself was not able to take." A curious proviso, Abner thought. But then everything about Grandfather Whateley had been strange, as if the decadence of Dunwich had infected him irrevocably.

And nothing was stranger than that Abner Whateley should come back from his cosmopolitan way of life to heed his grandfather's adjurations for property which was scarcely worth the time and trouble it would take to dispose of it. He reflected ruefully that such relatives as still lived in or near Dunwich might well resent his return in their curious inward-growing and isolated rustication which had kept most of the Whateleys in this immediate region, particularly since the shocking events which had overtaken the country branch of the family on Sentinel Hill.

The house appeared to be unchanged. The river side of the house was given over to the mill, which had long ago ceased to function, as more and more of the fields around Dunwich had grown barren; except for one room above the mill wheel—Aunt Sarey's room—the entire side of the structure bordering the Miskatonic had been abandoned even in the time of his boyhood, when Abner Whateley had last visited his grandfather, then living alone in the house except for the never-seen Aunt Sarey, who abode in her shuttered room with her door locked, never to move about the house under prohibition of such movement by her father, from whose domination only death at last had freed her.

A veranda, fallen in at the corner of the house, circled that part of the structure used as a dwelling; from the lattice-work under the eaves great cobwebs hung, undisturbed by anything save the wind for years. And dust lay over everything, inside as well as out, as Abner discovered when he had found the right key among the lot the lawyer had sent him. He found a lamp and lit it, for Grandfather Whateley had scorned electricity. In the yellow glow of light, the familiarity of the old kitchen with its nineteenth-century appointments smote him like a blow. Its spareness, the hand-hewn table and chairs, the century-old clock on the mantel, the worn broom—all were tangible reminders of his fear-haunted childhood visits to this formidable house and its even more formidable occupant, his mother's aged father.

The lamplight disclosed something more. On the kitchen table lay an envelope addressed to him in handwriting so crabbed that it could only be that of a very old or infirm man—his grandfather. Without troubling to bring the rest of his things from the car, Abner sat down to the table, blowing the dust off the chair and sufficiently from the table to allow him a resting place for his elbows, and opened the envelope.

The spidery script leaped out at him. The words were as severe as he remembered his grandfather to have been. And abrupt, with no term of endearment, not even the prosaic form of greeting.

Grandson:

When you read this, I will be some months dead. Perhaps more, unless they find you sooner than I believe they will. I have left you a sum of money—all I have and die possessed of—which is in the bank at Arkham under your name now. I do this not alone because you are my one and only grandson but because among all the Whateleys—we are an accursed clan, my boy—you have gone forth into the world and gathered to yourself learning sufficient to permit you to look upon all things with an inquiring mind ridden neither by the superstition of ignorance nor the superstition of science. You will understand my meaning.

It is my wish that at least the mill section of this house be destroyed. Let it be taken apart, board by board. If anything in it lives, I adjure you solemnly to kill it. No matter how small it may be. No matter what form it may have, for if it seems to you human it will beguile you and endanger your life and God knows how many others.

Heed me in this.

If I seem to have the sound of madness, pray recall that worse than madness has spawned among the Whateleys. I have stood free of it. It has not been so of all that is mine. There is more stubborn madness in those who are unwilling to believe in what they know not of and deny that such exists, than in those of our blood who have been guilty of terrible practices, and blasphemy against God, and worse.

Your grandfather, Luther S. Whateley.

How like Grandfather! thought Abner. He remembered, spurred into memory by this enigmatic, self-righteous communication, how on one occasion when his mother had mentioned her sister Sarah, and clapped her fingers across her mouth in dismay, he had run to his grandfather to ask,

"Grandpa, where's Aunt Sarey?"

The old man had looked at him out of eyes that were basilisk and answered, "Boy, we do not speak of Sarah here."

Aunt Sarey had offended the old man in some dreadful way—dreadful, at least, to that firm disciplinarian—for from that time, beyond even Abner Whateley's memory, his aunt had been only the name of a woman, who was his mother's oldest sister, and who was locked in the big room over the mill and kept forever invisible within those walls, behind the shutters nailed to her windows. It had been forbidden both Abner and his mother even to linger before the door of that shuttered room, though on one occasion Abner had crept up to the door and put his ear against it to listen to the snuffling and whimpering sounds that went on inside, as from some large person, and Aunt Sarey, he had decided, must be as large as a circus fat lady, for she devoured so much, judging by the great platters of food—chiefly meat, which she must have prepared herself, since so much of it was raw—carried to the room twice daily by old Luther Whateley himself, for there were no servants in that house, and had not been since the time Abner's mother had married, after Aunt Sarey had come back, strange and mazed, from a visit to distant kin in Innsmouth. He refolded the letter and put it back into the envelope. He would think of its contents another day. His first need now was to make sure of a place to sleep. He went out and got his two remaining bags from the car and brought them to the kitchen. Then he picked up the lamp and went into the interior of the house. The old-fashioned parlor, which was always kept closed against that day when visitors came—and none save Whateleys called upon Whateleys in Dunwich—he ignored. He made his way instead to his grandfather's bedroom; it was fitting that he should occupy the old man's bed now that he, and not Luther Whateley, was master here.

The large double bed was covered with faded copies of the *Arkham Advertiser,* carefully arranged to protect the fine cloth of the spread, which had been embossed with an armigerous design, doubtless a legitimate Whateley heritage. He set down the lamp and cleared away the newspapers. When he turned down the bed, he saw that it was clean and fresh, ready for occupation; some cousin of his grandfather's had doubtless seen to this, against his arrival, after the obsequies.

Then he got his bags and transferred them to the bedroom, which was in that corner of the house away from the village; its windows looked along the river, though they were more than the width of the mill from the bank of the stream. He opened the only one of them which had a screen across its lower half, then sat down on the edge of the bed, bemused, pondering the circumstances which had brought him back to Dunwich after all these years.

He was tired now. The heavy traffic around Boston had tired him. The contrast between the Boston region and this desolate Dunwich country depressed and troubled him. Moreover, he was conscious of an intangible uneasiness. If he had not had need of his legacy to continue his research abroad into the ancient civilizations of the South Pacific, he would never have come here. Yet family ties existed, for all that he would deny them. Grim and forbidding as old Luther Whateley had always been, he was his mother's father, and to him his grandson owed the allegiance of common blood.

Round Mountain loomed close outside the bedroom; he felt its presence as he had when a boy, sleeping in the room above. Trees, for long untended, pressed upon the house, and from one of them at this hour of deep dusk, a screech owl's bell-like notes dropped into the still summer air. He lay back for a moment, strangely lulled by the owl's pleasant song. A thousand thoughts crowded upon him, a myriad memories. He saw himself again as the little boy he was, always half-fearful of enjoying himself in these foreboding surroundings, always happy to come and happier to leave.

But he could not lie here, however relaxing it was. There was so much to be done before he could hope to take his departure that he could ill afford to indulge himself in rest and make a poor beginning of his nebulous obligation. He swung himself off the bed, picked up the lamp again, and began a tour of the house.

He went from the bedroom to the dining room, which was situated between it and the kitchen—a room of stiff, uncomfortable furniture, also handmade—and from there across to the parlor, the door of which opened upon a world far closer in its furniture and decorations to the eighteenth century than to the nineteenth, and far removed from the twentieth. The absence of dust testified to the tightness of the doors closing the room off from the rest of the house. He went up the open stairs to the floor above, from bedroom to bedroom—all dusty, with faded curtains, and showing every sign of having remained unoccupied for many years even before old Luther Whateley died.

Then he came to the passage which led to the shuttered room—Aunt Sarey's hideaway—or prison—he could now never learn what it might have been, and, on impulse, he went down and stood before that forbidden door. No snuffling, no whimpering greeted him now—nothing at all, as he stood before it, remembering, still caught in the spell of the prohibition laid upon him by his grandfather.

But there was no longer any reason to remain under that adjuration. He pulled out the ring of keys, and patiently tried one. He unlocked the door and pushed; it swung protestingly open. He held the lamp high.

He had expected to find a lady's boudoir, but the shuttered room was startling in its condition—bedding scattered about, pillows on the floor, the remains of food dried on a huge platter hidden behind a bureau. An odd, ichthic smell pervaded the room, rushing at him with such musty strength that he could hardly repress a gasp of disgust. The room was in shambles; moreover, it wore the aspect of having been in such wild disorder for a long, long time.

Abner put the lamp on a bureau drawn away from the wall, crossed to the window above the mill wheel, unlocked it, and raised it. He strove to open the shutters before he remembered that they had been nailed shut. Then he stood back, raised his foot, and kicked the shutters out to let a welcome blast of fresh, damp air into the room.

He went around to the adjoining outer wall and broke away

the shutters from the single window in that wall, as well. It was not until he stood back to survey his work that he noticed he had broken a small corner out of the pane of the window above the mill wheel. His quick regret was as quickly repressed in the memory of his grandfather's insistence that the mill and this room above it be torn down or otherwise destroyed. What mattered a broken pane!

He returned to take up the lamp again. As he did so, he gave the bureau a shove to push it back against the wall once more. At the same moment he heard a small rustling sound along the baseboard and, looking down, caught sight of a long-legged frog or toad—he could not make out which—vanishing under the bureau. He was tempted to rout the creature out, but he reflected that its presence could not matter—if it had existed in these locked quarters for so long on such cockroaches and other insects as it had managed to uncover, it merited being left alone.

He went out of the room, locked the door again, and returned to the master bedroom downstairs. He felt, obscurely, that he had made a beginning, however trivial; he had scouted the ground, so to speak. And he was twice as tired for his brief look around as he had been before. Though the hour was not late, he decided to go to bed and get an early start in the morning. There was the old mill yet to be gone through—perhaps some of the machinery could be sold, if any remained—and the mill wheel was now a curiosity, having continued to exist beyond its time.

He stood for a few minutes on the veranda, marking with surprise the welling stridulation of the crickets and katydids, and the almost overwhelming choir of the whippoorwills and frogs, which rose on all sides to assault him with a deafening insistence of such proportion as to drown out all other sounds, even such as might have risen from Dunwich. He stood there until he could tolerate the voices of the night no longer; then he retreated, locking the door, and made his way to the bedroom.

He undressed and got into bed, but he did not sleep for almost an hour, bedeviled by the chorus of natural sounds outside the house and from within himself by a rising confusion about what his grandfather had meant by the "dissolution" he himself had not been able to make. But at last he drifted into a troubled sleep.

II

He woke with the dawn, little rested. All night he had dreamed of strange places and beings that filled him with beauty and wonder and dread—of swimming in the ocean's depths and up the Miskatonic among fish and amphibia and strange men, half batrachian in aspect—of monstrous entities that lay sleeping in an eerie stone city at the bottom of the sea—of utterly outré music as of flutes accompanied by weird ululations from throats far, far from human—of Grandfather Luther Whateley standing accusingly before him and thundering forth his wrath at him for having dared to enter Aunt Sarey's shuttered room.

He was troubled, but he shrugged his unease away before the necessity of walking into Dunwich for the provisions he had neglected to bring with him in his haste. The morning was bright and sunny; peewees and thrushes sang, and dew pearled on leaf and blade reflected the sunlight in a thousand jewels along the winding path that led to the main street of the village. As he went along, his spirits rose; he whistled happily and contemplated the early fulfillment of his obligation, upon which his escape from this desolate, forgotten pocket of ingrown humanity was predicted.

But the main street of Dunwich was no more reassuring under the light of the sun than it had been in the dusk of the past evening. The village huddled between the Miskatonic and the almost vertical slope of Round Mountain, a dark and brooding settlement which seemed somehow never to have passed 1900, as if time had ground to a stop before the turn of the last century. His gay whistle faltered and died away; he averted his eyes from the buildings falling into ruin; he avoided the curiously expressionless faces of passersby and went directly to the old church with its general store, which he knew he would find slovenly and ill-kept, in keeping with the village itself.

A gaunt-faced storekeeper watched his advance down the aisle, searching his features for any familiar lineament.

Abner strode up to him and asked for bacon, coffee, eggs, and milk.

The storekeeper peered at him. He made no move. "Ye'll be a Whateley," he said at last. "I don't expeck ye know me. I'm yer cousin Tobias. Which one uv 'em are ye?"

"I'm Abner—Luther's grandson." He spoke reluctantly.

Tobias Whateley's face froze. "Libby's boy—Libby that married Cousin Jeremiah. Yew folks ain't back—back at Luther's? Yew folks ain't a-goin' to start things again?"

"There's no one but me," said Abner shortly. "What things are you talking about?"

"If ye dun't know, 'taint fer me to say."

Nor would Tobias Whateley speak again. He put together what Abner wanted, took his money sullenly, and watched him out of the store with ill-concealed animosity.

Abner was disagreeably affected. The brightness of the morning had dimmed for him, though the sun shone from the same unclouded heaven. He hastened away from the store and main street and hurried along the lane toward the house he had but recently quitted.

He was even more disturbed to discover, standing before the house, an ancient rig drawn by an old work-horse. Beside it stood a boy, and inside it sat an old, white-bearded man, who, at sight of Abner's approach, signaled to the boy for assistance, and by the lad's aid, laboriously descended to the ground and stood to await Abner.

As Abner came up, the boy spoke, unsmiling. "Great-Grampa'll talk to yew."

"Abner," said the old man quaveringly, and Abner saw for the first time how very old he was.

"This here's Great-Grampa Zebulon Whateley," said the boy.

Grandfather Luther Whateley's brother—the only living Whateley of his generation.

"Come in, sir," said Abner, offering the old man his arm.

Zebulon Whateley took it.

The three of them made slow progress toward the veranda, where the old man halted at the foot of the steps, turning his dark eyes upon Abner from under their bushy white brows, and shaking his head gently.

"Naow, if yo'll fetch me a cheer, I'll set."

"Bring a chair from the kitchen, boy," said Abner.

The boy sped up the steps and into the house. He was out as fast with a chair for the old man, and helped to lower him to it, and stood beside him while Zebulon Whateley caught his breath.

Presently he turned his eyes full upon Abner and contemplated him, taking in every detail of his clothes, which, unlike his own, were not made by hand.

"Why have ye come, Abner?" he asked, his voice firmer now.

Abner told him, as simply and directly as he could.

Zebulon Whateley shook his head. "Ye know no more'n the rest, and less'n some," he said. "What Luther was abaout, only God knowed. Naow Luther's gone, and ye'll have it to dew. I kin tell ye, Abner, I vaow after God, I don't know why Luther took on so and locked hisself up and Sarey that time she come back from Innsmouth—but I kin say it was suthin' turrible, turrible—and the things what happened was turrible. Ain't nobody left to say Luther was to blame, nor poor Sarey—but take care, take care, Abner."

"I expect to follow my grandfather's wishes," said Abner.

The old man nodded. But his eyes were troubled, and it was plain that he had little faith in Abner.

"How'd you find out I was here, Uncle Zebulon?" Abner asked.

"I had the word ye'd come. It was my bounden duty to talk to ye. The Whateleys has a curse on 'em. That's been them naow gone to graoun' has had to dew with the devil, and thar's some what whistled turrible thing aout o' the air, and thar's some what had to dew with things that wasn't all human nor all fish but lived in the water and swum aout—way aout—to sea, and thar's some what growed in on themselves and got all mazed and queer—and that's what happened on Sentinel Hill that time—Lavinny's Wilbur—and that other one by the Sentinel Stone—Gawd, I shake when I think on it. . . ."

"Now, Grampa—don't ye git yer dander up," chided the boy.

"I wun't, I wun't," said the old man tremulously. "It's all died away naow. It's forgot—by all but me and them what took the signs daown—the signs that pointed to Dunwich, sayin' it was too turrible a place to know about. . . ." He shook his head and was silent.

"Uncle Zebulon," said Abner, "I never saw my Aunt Sarah."

"No, no, boy—she was locked up that time. Afore you was borned, I think it was."

"Why?"

"Only Luther knowed—and Gawd. Now Luther's gone, and Gawd dun't seem like He knowed Dunwich is still here."

"What was Aunt Sarah doing in Innsmouth?"

"Visitin' kin."

"Are there Whateleys there, too?"

"Not Whateleys. Marshes. Old Obed Marsh that was Pa's cousin. Him and his wife that he found in the trade—at Ponape, if ye know what that is."

"I do."

"Ye dew? I never knowed. They say Sarey was visitin' Marsh kin—Obed's son or grandson—I never knowed which. Never heerd. Dun't care. She was thar quite a spell. They say when she come back she was different. Flighty. Unsettled. Sassed her pa. And than, not long after, he locked her up in that room till she died."

"How long after?"

"Three, four months. And Luther never said what fer. Nobody

saw her again after that till the day she wuz laid aout in her coffin. Two year, might be three year ago. Thar was that time nigh onto a year after she come back from Innsmouth thar was sech goin's-on here at this house—a-fightin' and a-screamin' and a-screechin'—most everyone in Dunwich heerd it, but no one went to see what it was, and next day Luther he said it was only Sarey took with a spell. Might be it was. Might be it was suthin' else . . ."

"*What* else, Uncle Zebulon?"

"Devil's work," said the old man instantly. "But I fergit—ye're the eddicated one. Ain't many Whateleys ever bin eddicated. Thar was Lavinny—she read them turrible books what was no good for her. And Sarey—she read some. Them as has only a little learnin' might's well have none—they ain't fit to handle life with only a little learnin', they're fitter with none a-tall."

Abner smiled.

"Dun't ye laugh, boy!"

"I'm not laughin, Uncle Zebulon. I agree with you."

"Then if ye come face to face with it, ye'll know what to dew. Ye won't stop and think—ye'll just dew."

"With what?"

"I wisht I knowed, Abner. I don't. Gawd knows. Luther knowed. Luther's dead. It comes on me Sarey knowed, too. Sarey's dead. Now nobody knows what terrible thing it was. Ef I was a prayin' man, I'd pray you don't find aout—but if ye dew, dun't stop to figger it aout by eddication, jest dew whut ye have to dew. Yer Grandpa kep' a record—look fer it. Ye might learn what kind a people the Marshes was—they wasn't like us—suthin' turrible happened to 'em—and might be it reached aout and tetched Sarey. . . ."

Something stood between the old man and Abner Whateley—something unvoiced, perhaps unknown, but it was something that cast a chill about Abner for all his conscious attempt to belittle what he felt.

"I'll learn what I can, Uncle Zebulon," he promised.

The old man nodded and beckoned to the boy. He signified that he wished to rise, to return to the buggy. The boy came running.

"Ef ye need me, Abner, send word to Tobias," said Zebulon Whateley. "I'll come—ef I can."

"Thank you."

Abner and the boy helped the old man back into the buggy. Zebulon Whateley raised his forearm in a gesture of farewell, the boy whipped up the horse, and the buggy drew away.

Abner stood for a moment looking after the departing vehicle. He was both troubled and irritated—troubled at the suggestion of something dreadful which lurked beneath Zebulon Whateley's words of warning, irritated because his grandfather, despite all his adjurations, had left him so little to act upon. Yet this must have been because his grandfather evidently believed there might be nothing untoward to greet his grandson when at last Abner Whateley arrived at the old house. It could be nothing other by way of explanation.

Yet Abner was not entirely convinced. Was the matter one of such horror that Abner should not know of it unless he had to? Or had Luther Whateley laid down a key to the riddle elsewhere in the house? He doubted it. It would not be Grandfather's way to seek the devious when he had always been so blunt and direct.

He went into the house with his groceries, put them away, and sat down to map out a plan of action. The very first thing to be accomplished was a survey of the mill part of the structure, to determine whether any machinery could be salvaged. Next he must find someone who would undertake to tear down the mill and the room above it. Thereafter he must dispose of the house and adjoining property, though he had a sinking feeling of futility at the conviction that he would never find anyone who would want to settle in so forlorn a corner of Massachusetts as Dunwich.

He began at once to carry out his obligations.

His search of the mill, however, disclosed that the machinery which had been in it—save for such pieces as were fixed to the running of the wheel—had been removed and, presumably, sold. Perhaps the increment from the sale was part of that very legacy Luther Whateley had deposited in the bank at Arkham for his grandson. Abner was spared the necessity of removing the machinery before beginning the planned demolition. The dust in the old mill almost suffocated him; it lay an inch thick over everything, and it rose in great gusts to cloud about him when he walked through the empty, cobwebbed rooms. Dust muffled his footsteps, and he was glad to leave the mill to go around and look at the wheel.

He worked his way around the wooden ledge to the frame of the wheel, somewhat uncertain, lest the wood give way and plunge him into the water beneath; but the construction was firm, the wood did not give, and he was soon at the wheel. It appeared to be a splendid example of middle-nineteenth-century work. It would be a shame to tear it apart, thought Abner. Perhaps the wheel could be removed, and a place could be found for it either in some museum or in some one of those buildings which were forever being reconstructed by wealthy persons interested in the preservation of the American heritage.

He was about to turn away from the wheel, when his eye was caught by a series of small wet prints on the paddles. He bent closer to examine them, but, apart from ascertaining that they were already in part dried, he could not see in them more than marks left by some small animal, probably batrachian—a frog or a toad—which had apparently mounted the wheel in the early hours before the rising of the sun. His eyes, rising, followed the line of the wheel to the broken-out shutters of the room above.

He stood for a moment, thinking. He recalled the batrachian creature he had glimpsed along the baseboard of the shuttered room. Perhaps it had escaped through the broken pane? Or, more likely, perhaps another of its kind had discovered its presence and gone up to it. A faint apprehension stirred in him, but he brushed it away in irritation that a man of his intelligence should have been sufficiently stirred by the aura of ignorant, superstitious mystery clinging to his grandfather's memory to respond to it.

Nevertheless, he went around and mounted the stairs to the shuttered room. He half expected, when he unlocked the door, to find some significant change in the aspect of the room as he remembered it from last night, but, apart from the unaccustomed daylight streaming into the room, there was no alteration.

He crossed to the window.

There were prints on the sill. There were two sets of them. One appeared to be leading out, the other entering. They were not the same size. The prints leading outward were tiny, only half an inch across. Those leading in were double that size. Abner bent close and stared at them in fixed fascination.

He was not a zoologist, but he was by no means ignorant of zoology. The prints on the sill were like nothing he had ever seen before, not even in a dream. Save for being or seeming to be webbed, they were the perfect prints in miniature of human hands and feet.

Though he made a cursory search for the creature, he saw no sign of it, and finally, somewhat shaken, he retreated from the room and locked the door behind him, already regretting the impulse which had led him to it in the first place and which had caused him to burst open the shutters which for so long had walled the room away from the outer world.

III

He was not entirely surprised to learn that no one in Dunwich could be found to undertake the demolition of the mill. Even such carpenters as those who had not worked for a long time were reluctant to undertake the task, pleading a variety of excuses, which Abner easily recognized as a disguise for the superstitious fear of the place under which one and all labored. He found it necessary to drive into Aylesbury, but though he encountered no difficulty in engaging a trio of husky young men who had formed a partnership to tear down the mill, he was forced to wait upon their previous commitments and had to return to Dunwich with the promise that they would come "in a week or ten days."

Thereupon he set about at once to examine into all the effects of Luther Whateley which still remained in the house. There were stacks of newspapers—chiefly the *Arkham Advertiser* and the *Aylesbury Transcript*—now yellowing with age and moldering with dust, which he set aside for burning. There were books which he determined to go over individually in order that he might not destroy anything of value. And there were letters which he would have burned at once had he not happened to glance into one of them and catch sight of the name "Marsh," at which he read on.

Luther, what happened to Cousin Obed is a singular thing. I do not know how to tell it to you. I do not know how to make it credible. I am not sure I have all the facts in this matter. I cannot believe but that it is a rigmarole deliberately invented to conceal something of a scandalous nature, for you know the Marshes have always been given to exaggeration and had a pronounced flair for deception. Their ways are devious. They have always been.

But the story, as I have it from Cousin Alizah, is that when he was a young man Obed and some others from Innsmouth, sailing their trading ships into the Polynesian Islands, encountered there a strange people who called themselves the "Deep Ones" and who had the ability to live either in the water or on the earth. Amphibians, they would then be. Does this sound credible to you? It does not to me. What is most astonishing is that Obed, and some others, married women of these people and brought them home to live with them.

Now that is the legend. *Here are the* facts. *Ever since that time, the Marshes have prospered mightily in the trade. Mrs. Marsh is never seen abroad, save on such occasions as she goes to certain closed affairs of the Order of Dagon Hall. Dagon is said to be a sea god. I know nothing of these pagan religions, and wish to know nothing. The Marsh children have* a very strange *look. I do not exaggerate, Luther, when I tell you that they have such wide mouths and such chinless faces and such large staring eyes that I swear they sometimes look more like frogs than human beings! They are not, at least as far as I can see,* gilled. *The Deep Ones are said to be possessed of gills, and to belong to Dagon or to some other deity of the sea whose name I cannot even pronounce, far less set down. No matter. It is such a rigmarole as the Marshes might well invent to serve their purposes, but, by God, Luther, judging by the way the ships Captain Marsh has in the East India trade keep afloat without a smitchin of damage done to them by storm or wear—the brigantine* Columbia, *the barque* Sumatra Queen, *the brig* Hetty, *and some others—it might also seem that he has made some sort of bargain with Neptune himself!*

Then there are all the doings off the coast where the Marshes live. Night swimming. They swim way out off Devil Reef, which, as you know, is a mile and a half out from the harbor here at Innsmouth. People keep away from the Marshes—except the Martins and some such others among them who were also in the East India trade. Now that Obed is gone—and I suppose Mrs. Marsh may be also, since she is no longer seen anywhere—the children and the grandchildren of old Captain Obed follow in his strange ways.

The letter dwindled down to commonplaces about prices—ridiculously low figures seen from this vantage of over half a century later, for Luther Whateley must have been a young man, unmarried, at the time this letter had been written to him by Ariah, a cousin of whom Abner had never heard. What it had to say of the Marshes was nothing—or all, perhaps, if Abner had the key to the puzzle of which, he began to believe with mounting irritation, he held only certain disassociated parts.

But if Luther Whateley had believed this rigmarole, would he, years later, have permitted his daughter to visit the Marsh cousins? Abner doubted it.

He went through other letters—bills, receipts, trivial accounts of journeys made to Boston, Newburyport, Kingsport—postcards, and came at last to another letter from Cousin Ariah, written, if a comparison of dates was sufficient evidence, immediately after the one Abner had just read. They were ten days apart, and Luther would have had time to reply to that first.

Abner opened it eagerly.

The first page was an account of certain small family matters pertinent to the marriage of another cousin, evidently a sister of Ariah; the second a speculation about the future of the East India trade, with a paragraph about a new book by Whitman—evidently Walt; but the third was manifestly in answer to something Grandfather Whateley had evidently written concerning the Marsh branch of the family.

Well, Luther, you may be right in this matter of race prejudice as responsible for the feeling against the Marshes. I know how people here feel about other races. It is unfortunate, perhaps, but such is their lack of education that they find much room for such prejudices. But I am not convinced that it is all *due to race prejudice. I don't know what kind of race it is that would give the Marshes after Obed that strange* look. *The East India people—such as I have seen and recall from my early days in the trade—have features much like our own, and only a different color to the skin—copper, I would call it. Once I did see a native who had a similar appearance, but he was evidently not typical, for he was shunned by all the workers around the ships in the harbor where I saw him. I've forgotten now where it was, but I think Ponape.*

To give them their due, the Marshes keep pretty much to themselves—or to those families living here under the same cloud. And they more or less run the town. It may be significant—it may have been accident—that one selectman who spoke out against them was found drowned soon after. I am the first to admit that coincidences more startling than this frequently occur, but you may be sure that people who disliked the Marshes made the most of this.

But I know how your analytical mind is cold to such talk; I will spare you more of it.

Thereafter not a word. Abner went through bundles of letters in vain. What Ariah wrote in subsequent letters dealt scrupulously with family matters of the utmost triviality. Luther Whateley had evidently made his displeasure with mere gossip clear; even as a young man, Luther must have been strictly self-disciplined. Abner found but one further reference to any mystery at Innsmouth—that was a newspaper clipping dealing in very vague terms, suggesting that the reporter who sent in the story did not really know what had taken place, with certain Federal activity in and near Innsmouth in 1928—the attempted destruction of Devil Reef, and the blowing up of large sections of the waterfront, together with wholesale arrests of Marshes and Martins and some others. But this event was decades removed from Ariah's early letters.

Abner put the letters dealing with the Marshes into his pocket and summarily burned the rest, taking the mass of material he had gone through out along the riverbank and setting fire to it. He stood guarding it, lest a chance wind carry a spark to surrounding grass, which was unseasonably dry. He welcomed the smell of the smoke, however, for a certain dead odor lingered along the riverbank, rising from the remains of fish upon which some animal had feasted—an otter, he thought.

As he stood beside the fire, his eyes roved over the old Whateley building, and he saw with a rueful reflection that it was high time the mill was coming down, that several panes of the window he had broken in the rooms that had been Aunt Sarey's, together with a portion of the frame, had fallen out. Fragments of the window were scattered on the paddles of the mill wheel.

By the time the fire was sufficiently low to permit his leaving it, the day was drawing to a close. He ate a meager supper and, having had his fill of reading for the day, decided against attempting to turn up his grandfather's "record," of which Uncle Zebulon Whateley had spoken, and went out to watch the dusk and the night from the veranda, hearing again the rising chorus of the frogs and whippoorwills.

He retired early, unwontedly weary.

Sleep, however, would not come. For one thing, the summer night was warm; hardly a breath of air stirred. For another, even above the ululation of the frogs and the demoniac insistence of the whippoorwills, sounds from within the house invaded his consciousness—the creaks and groans of a many-timbered house settling in for the night; a peculiar scuffling or shuffling sound, half-drag, half-hop, that Abner laid to rats, which must abound in the mill section of the structure—and indeed, the noises were muffled and seemed to reach him as from some distance; and, at one time, the cracking of wood and the tinkle of glass, which, Abner guessed, very probably came from the window above the mill wheel. The house was virtually falling to pieces about him; it was as if he served as a catalytic agent to bring about the final dissolution of the old structure.

This concept amused him because it struck him that, willy-nilly, he was carrying out his grandfather's adjuration. And, so bemused, he fell asleep.

He was awakened early in the morning by the ringing of the telephone, which he had had the foresight to have connected for the duration of his visit to Dunwich. He had already taken down the receiver from the ancient instrument attached to the wall before he realized that the call was on a party line and not intended for him. Nevertheless, the woman's voice that leaped out at him burst open his ear with such screaming insistence that he remained frozen to the telephone.

"I tell ye, Mis' Corey, I *heard* things las' night—the graoun' was a-talkin' agen, and along abaout midnight I heard that scream—I never figgered a caow'd scream that way—jest like a rabbit, only deeper. That was Lutey Sawyer's cow—they faoun' her this morning—more'n haff et by animals. . . ."

"Mis' Bishop, you dun't s'pose . . . it's come back?"

"I dun't know. I hope t' Gawd it ain't. But it's the same as the las' time."

"Was it jest that one caow took?"

"Jes the one. I ain't heerd abaout no more. But that's how it begun the las' time, Mis' Corey."

Quietly, Abner replaced the receiver. He smiled grimly at this evidence of the rampant superstitions of the Dunwich natives. He had never really known the depths of ignorance and superstition in which dwellers in such out-of-the-way places as Dunwich lived, and this manifestation of it was, he was convinced, but a mild sample.

He had little time, however, to dwell upon the subject, for he had to go into town for fresh milk, and he strode forth into the morning of sun and clouds with a certain feeling of relief at such brief escape from the house.

Tobias Whateley was uncommonly sullen and silent at Abner's entrance. Abner sensed not only resentment, but a certain tangible fear. He was astonished. To all Abner's comments, Tobias replied in muttered monosyllables. Thinking to make conversation, he began to tell Tobias what he had overheard on the party line.

"I know it," said Tobias, curtly, for the first time gazing at Abner's face with naked terror.

Abner was stunned into silence. Terror vied with animosity in Tobias' eyes. His feelings were plain to Abner before he dropped his gaze and took the money Abner offered in payment.

"Yew seen Zebulon?" he asked in a low voice.

"He was at the house," said Abner.

"Yew talk to him?"

"We talked."

It seemed as if Tobias expected that certain matters had passed between them, but there was that in his attitude that suggested he was puzzled by subsequent events, which seemed to indicate that Zebulon had not told him what Tobias had expected the old man to tell him, or else that Abner had disregarded some of his uncle's advice. Abner began to feel completely mystified; added to the superstitious talk of the natives on the telephone, to the strange hints Uncle Zebulon had dropped, this attitude of his cousin Tobias filled him with utter perplexity. Tobias, no more than Zebulon, seemed inclined to come out frankly and put into words what lay behind his sullen features—each acted as if Abner, as a matter of course, should know.

In his bafflement, he left the store and walked back to the Whateley house determined to hasten his tasks as much as he could so that he might get away from this forgotten hamlet with its queer, superstition-ridden people, for all that many of them were his relatives.

To that end, he returned to the task of sorting his grandfather's things as soon as he had had his breakfast, of which he ate very little, for his disagreeable visit to the store had dulled the appetite which he had felt when he had set out for the store earlier.

It was not until late afternoon that he found the record he sought—an old ledger, in which Luther Whateley had made certain entries in his crabbed hand.

IV

By the light of the lamp, Abner sat down to the kitchen table after he had had a small repast, and opened Luther Whateley's ledger. The opening page had been torn out, but from an examination of the fragments of sheets still attached to the threads of the sewing, Abner concluded that these pages were purely of accounts, as if his grandfather had taken up an old, not completely used account book for a purpose other than keeping accounts, and had removed such sheets as had been more prosaically utilized.

From the beginning, the entries were cryptic. They were undated, except for the day of the week.

"This Saturday Ariah answered my inquiry. S. was seen sev. times with Ralsa Marsh. Obed's great-grandson. *Swam* together by night."

Such was the first entry, clearly pertaining to Aunt Sarey's visit to Innsmouth, about which Grandfather had plainly inquired of Ariah. Something had impelled Luther to make such inquiry. From what he knew of his grandfather's character, Abner concluded that the inquiry had been made after Sarey had returned to Dunwich.

Why?

The next story was pasted in, and was clearly part of a typewritten letter received by Luther Whateley.

Ralsa Marsh is probably the most repellent of all the family. He is almost degenerate *in his looks. I know you have said that it was Libby of your daughters who was the fairest; even so, we cannot imagine how Sarah came to take up with someone who is so repulsive as Ralsa, in whom all those recessive characteristics which have been seen in the Marsh family after Obed's strange marriage to that Polynesian woman (the Marshes have denied that Obed's wife was Polynesian, but of course he was trading there at that time, and I don't credit those stories about that uncharted island where he was supposed to have dallied) seem to have come to fullest fruit.*

As far as I can now ascertain—after all, it is over two months—close to four, I think, since her return to Dunwich—they were constantly together. I am surprised that Ariah did not inform you of this. None of us here had any mandate to halt Sarah's seeing Ralsa, and, after all, they are cousins and she was visiting at the Marshes'—not here.

Abner judged that this letter had been written by a woman, also a cousin, who bore Luther some resentment for Sarah's not having been sent to stay with her branch of the family. Luther had evidently made inquiry of her regarding Ralsa.

The third entry was once again in Luther's hand, summarizing a letter from Ariah.

Saturday, Ariah maintains Deep Ones—a sect of quasi-religious group. Subhuman. Said to live in the sea and worship Dagon. Another God named Cthulhu. Gilled people. Resembling frogs or toads more than fish, but eyes ichthic. Claims Obed's late wife was one. Holds that Obed's children all bore the marks. Marshes gilled? How else could they swim a mile and a half to Devil Reef, and back? Marshes eat sparingly, can go without food and drink a long time, diminish or expand in size rapidly. (To this Luther had appended four scornful exclamation marks.)

Zadok Allen swears he saw Sarah swimming out to Devil Reef. Marshes carrying her along. All naked. *Swears he saw Marshes with tough, warty skin. Some with* scales, *like fish! Swears he saw them chase and eat fish! Tear them apart like animals.*

The next entry was again a portion of a letter, patently a reply to one from Grandfather Whateley.

You aks who is responsible for those ridiculous *tales about the Marshes. Well, Luther, it would be impossible to single out any one of a dozen people over several generations. I agree that old Zadok Allen talks too much, drinks, and may be romancing. But he is only one. The fact is this legend—or* rigmarole, *as you call it—has grown up from one generation to the next. Through three generations. You have only to look at some of the descendants of Captain Obed to understand why this could have come about. There are some Marsh offspring said to have been too horrible to look upon. Old wives' tales? Well, Dr. Rowley Marsh was too ill to attend one of the Marsh women one time; so they had to call Dr. Gilman, and Gilman always said that what he delivered was less than human. And nobody ever saw that particular Marsh, though there were people later who claimed to have seen* things moving on two legs that weren't human.

Following this there was but a brief but revealing entry in two words: "Punish Sarah."

This must then mark the date of Sarah Whateley's confinement to the room above the mill. For some time after this entry, there was no mention of his daughter in Luther's script. Instead, his jottings were not dated in any way, and judging by the difference in the color of the ink, were made at different times, though run together.

"Many frogs. Seem to bear in on the mill. Seem to be more than in the marshes across the Miskatonic. Sleeping difficult. Are whippoorwills on the increase, too, or is this imagination? . . . Counted thirty-seven frogs at the porch steps tonight."

There were more entries of this nature. Abner read them all, but there was no clue in them to what the old man had been getting at. Luther Whateley had thereafter kept book on frogs, fog, fish and their movements in the Miskatonic—when they rose and leaped from the water, and so on. This seemed to be unrelated data, and was not in any way connected to the problem of Sarah.

There was another hiatus after this series of notes, and then came a single, underscored entry.

"*Ariah was right!*"

But about *what* had Ariah been right? Abner wondered. And how had Luther Whateley learned that Ariah had been right? There was no evidence that Ariah and Luther had continued their correspondence, or even that Ariah desired to write to the crotchety Luther without a letter of direct inquiry from Luther.

There followed a section of the record to which newspaper clippings had been pasted. These were clearly unrelated, but they did establish for Abner the fact that somewhat better than a year had passed before Luther's next entry, one of the most puzzling Abner found. Indeed, the time hiatus seemed to be closer to two years.

"R. out again."

If Luther and Sarah were the only people in the house, who was "R."? Could it have been Ralsa Marsh come to visit? Abner doubted it, for there was nothing to show that Ralsa Marsh harbored any affection for his distant cousin, or certainly he would have pursued her before this.

The next notation seemed to be unrelated.

"Two turtles, one dog, remains of woodchuck. Bishop's—two cows, found on the Miskatonic end of the pasture."

A little further along, Luther had set down further such data.

"After one month a total of 17 cattle, 6 sheep. Hideous alterations; size commensurate with amt. of food. Z. over. Anxious about talk going around."

Could "Z." stand for Zebulon? Abner thought it did. Evidently then Zebulon had come in vain, for he had left him, Abner, with only vague and uncertain hints about the situation at the house when Aunt Sarey was confined to the shuttered room. Zebulon, on the evidence of such conversation as he had shared with Abner, knew less than Abner himself did after reading his grandfather's record. But he did know of Luther's record; so Luther must have told him he had set down certain facts.

These notations, however, were more in the nature of notes for something to be completed later; they were unaccountably cryptic, unless one had the key of basic knowledge which belonged to Luther Whateley. But a growing sense of urgency was clearly manifest in the old man's further entries.

"Ada Wilkerson gone. Trace of scuffle. Strong feeling in Dunwich. John Sawyer shook his fist at me—safely across the street, where I couldn't reach him."

"Monday. Howard Willie, this time. They found one shoe, with the foot still in it."

The record was now near its end. Many pages, unfortunately, had been detached from it—some with violence—but no clue remained as to why this violence had been done to Grandfather Whateley's account. It could not have been done by anyone but Luther himself; perhaps, thought Abner, Luther felt he had told too much, and intended to destroy anything which might put a later reader on the track of the true facts regarding Aunt Sarey's confinement for the rest of her life. He had certainly succeeded.

The next entry once again referred to the elusive "R."

"R. back at last."

Then, "Nailed the shutters to the windows of Sarah's room."

And at last: "Once he has lost weight, he must be kept on a careful diet and to a controllable size."

In a way, this was the most enigmatic entry of them all. Was "he" also "R."? If so, why must he be kept on a careful diet, and what did Luther Whateley mean by controlling his size? There was no ready answer to these questions in such material as Abner had read thus far, either in this record—or the fragmentary account still left in the record—or in letters previously perused.

He pushed away the record-book, resisting an impulse to burn it. He was exasperated, all the more so because he was uneasily aware of an urgent need to learn the secret embalmed within this old building.

The hour was now late; darkness had fallen some time ago, and the ever-present clamor of the frogs and the whippoorwills had begun once more, rising all around the house. Pushing from his thoughts briefly the apparently unconnected jottings he had been reading, he called from his memory the superstitions of the family, representing those prevalent in the countryside—associating frogs and the calling of whippoorwills and owls with death, and from this meditation progressed readily to the amphibian link which presented itself—the presence of the frogs brought before his mind's eye a grotesque caricature of one of the Marsh clan of Innsmouth, as described in the letters Luther Whateley had saved for so many years.

Oddly, this very thought, for all that it was so casual, startled him. The insistence of frogs and toads on singing and calling in the vicinity was truly remarkable. Yet, batrachia had always been plentiful in the Dunwich vicinity, and he had no way of knowing for how long a period before his arrival they had been calling about the old Whateley house. He discounted the suggestion that his arrival had anything at all to do with it; more than likely, the proximity of the Miskatonic and a low, swampy area immediately across the river on the edge of Dunwich accounted for the presence of so many frogs.

His exasperation faded away; his concern about the frogs did likewise. He was weary. He got up and put the record left by Luther Whateley carefully into one of his bags, intending to carry it away with him, and to puzzle over it until some sort of meaning came out of it. Somewhere there must exist a clue. If certain horrible events had taken place in the vicinity, something more in the way of a record must exist than Luther Whateley's spare notes. It would do no good to inquire of Dunwich people; Abner knew they would maintain a close-mouthed silence before an "outsider" like himself, for all that he was related to many of them.

It was then that he thought of the stacks of newspapers, still set aside to be burned. Despite his weariness, he began to go through packs of the *Aylesbury Transcript,* which carried, from time to time, a Dunwich department.

After an hour's hasty search, he found three vague articles, none of them in the regular Dunwich columns, which corroborated entries in Luther Whateley's ledger. The first appeared under the heading: WILD ANIMAL SLAYS STOCK NEAR DUNWICH—

Several cows and sheep have been slain on farms just outside Dunwich by what appears to be a wild animal of some kind. Traces left at the scenes of the slaughter suggest some large beast, but Professor Bethnall of Miskatonic University's anthropology department points out that it is not inconceivable that packs of wolves could lurk in the wild hill country around Dunwich. No beast of the size suggested by the traces reported was ever known to inhabit the Eastern Seaboard within the memory of man. County officials are investigating.

Search as he might, Abner could find no follow-up story. He did, however, come upon the story of Ada Wilkerson.

A widow-lady, Ada Wilkerson, 57, living along the Miskatonic out of Dunwich, may have been the victim of foul play three nights ago. When she failed to visit a friend by appointment in Dunwich, her home was visited. No trace of her was found. However, the door of her house had been broken in, and the furniture had been wildly thrown about, as if a violent struggle had taken place. A very strong musk is said to have pervaded the entire area. Up to press time today, Mrs. Wilkerson has not been heard from.

Two subsequent paragraphs reported briefly that authorites had not found any clue to Mrs. Wilkerson's disappearance. The account of a "large animal" was resurrected, lamely, and Professor Bethnall's beliefs on the possible existence of a wolf-pack, but nothing further, for investigation had disclosed that the missing lady had neither money nor enemies, and no one would have had any motive for killing her.

Finally, there was the account of Howard Willie's death, headed, SHOCKING CRIME AT DUNWICH.

Some time during the night of the twenty-first Howard Willie, 37, a native of Dunwich, was brutally slain as he was on his way home from a fishing trip, along the upper reaches of the Miskatonic. Mr. Willie was attacked about half a mile past the Luther Whateley property, as he walked through an arbored lane. He evidently put up a fierce fight, for the ground is badly torn up in all directions. The poor fellow was overcome, and must have been literally torn limb from limb, for the only physical remains of the victim consisted of his right foot, still encased in its shoe. It had evidently been cruelly torn from his leg by great force.

Our correspondent in Dunwich advises us that people there are very sullen and in a great rage of anger and fear. They suspect many of their number of being at least partly to blame, though they stoutly deny that anyone in Dunwich murdered either Willie or Mrs. Wilkerson, who disappeared a fortnight ago, and of whom no word has since been heard.

The account concluded with some data about Willie's family connections. Thereafter, subsequent editions of the *Transcript* were distinguished only for the lack of information about the events which had taken place in Dunwich, where authorities and reporters alike apparently ran up against blank walls in the stolid refusal of the natives to talk, or even speculate about what had happened. There was, however, one insistent note which recurred in the comments of investigators relayed to the press, and that was that such trail or track as could be seen appeared to have disappeared into the waters of the Miskatonic, suggesting that if an animal was responsible for the orgy of slaughter which had occurred at Dunwich, it may have come from and returned to the river.

Though it was now close to midnight, Abner massed the discarded newspapers together and took them out to the riverbank, where he set them on fire, having saved only torn pages relative to the occurrences at Dunwich. The air being still, he did not feel obliged to watch the fire, since he had already burned a considerable area, and the grass was not likely to catch on fire. As he started away, he heard suddenly above the ululation of the whippoorwills and frogs, now at a frenzied crescendo, the tearing and breaking sound of wood. He thought at once of the window of the shuttered room, and retraced his steps.

In the very dim light flickering toward the house from the burning newspapers, it seemed to Abner that the window gaped wider than before. Could it be that the entire mill part of the house was about to collapse? Then, out of the corner of his eye, he caught sight of a singularly formless moving shadow just beyond the mill wheel, and a moment later heard a churning sound in the water. The voices of the frogs had now risen to such a volume that he could hear nothing more.

He was inclined to dismiss the shadow as the creation of the wild flames leaping upward from the fire. The sound in the water might well have been that of the movement made by a school of fish, darting forward in concert. Nevertheless, he thought, it would do no harm to have another look at Aunt Sarey's room.

He returned to the kitchen, took the lamp, and mounted the stairs. He unlocked the door of the shuttered room, threw open the door, and was almost felled by the powerful musk which pushed hallward. The smell of the Miskatonic, of the marshes, the odors of that slimy deposit left on the stones and sunken debris when the Miskatonic receded to its low-water stage, the cloying pungence of some animal lairs—all these were combined in the shuttered room.

Abner stood for a moment, wavering on the threshold. True, the odor in the room could have come in through the open window. He raised the lamp so that more of its light fell upon the wall above the mill wheel. Even from where he stood, it was possible to see that not only was all the window itself now gone, but so was the frame. Even at this distance it was manifest that the frame had been broken out *from inside*!

He fell back, slammed the door shut, locked it, and fled downstairs with the shell of his rationalizations tumbling about him.

V

Downstairs, he fought for self-control. What he had seen was but one more detail added to the proliferating accumulation of seemingly unrelated data upon which he had stumbled ever since his coming to his grandfather's home. He was convinced now that, however unlikely it had at first seemed to him, all these data must be related. What he needed to learn was the one basic fact or element which bound them together.

He was badly shaken, particularly because he had the uneasy conviction that he did indeed have all the facts he needed to know, that it was his scientific training which made it impossible for him to make the primary assumption, to state the premise which the facts before him would inevitably prove. The evidence of his senses told him that something laired in that room—some bestial creature; it was folly to assume that odors from outside could so permeate Aunt Sarey's old room and not be noticeable outside the kitchen and at the windows of his own bedroom.

The habit of rational thinking was strong in him. He took out Luther Whateley's final letter to him once more and read it again. That was what his grandfather had meant when he had written,

". . . you have gone forth into the world and gathered to yourself learning sufficient to permit you to look upon all things with an inquiring mind ridden neither by the superstition of ignorance nor the superstition of science." Was this puzzle, with all its horrible connotations, beyond rationalization?

The wild ringing of the telephone broke in upon his confused thoughts. Slipping the letter back into his pocket, he strode rapidly to the wall and took the receiver off the hook.

A man's voice screamed over the wire, amid a chaos of inquiring voices as everyone on the line picked up his receiver as if they waited, like Abner Whateley himself, for word of another tragedy. One of the voices—all were disembodied and unidentifiable for Abner—identified the caller.

"It's Luke Lang!"

"Git a posse up an' come quick," Luke shouted hoarsely over the wire. "It's jest aoutside my door. Snufflin' araoun'. Tryin' the door. Feelin' at the winders."

"Luke, what *is* it?" asked a woman's voice.

"Oh, Gawd! It's some unairthly thing. It's a-hoppin' raoun' like it was too big to move right—like jelly. Oh, hurry, hurry, afore it's too late. It got my dog. . . ."

"Git off the wire so's we can call for help," interrupted another subscriber.

But Luke never heard in his extremity. "It's a-pushin' at the door—It's a-bowin' the door in. . . ."

"Luke! Luke! Git off'n the wire!"

"It's a-tryin the winder naow." Luke Lang's voice rose in a scream of terror. "There goes the glass. Gawd! Gawd! Hain't yew comin? Oh, that hand! That turr'ble arm! Gawd! that face . . . !"

Luke's voice died away in a frightful screech. There was the sound of breaking glass and rending wood—then all was still at Luke Lang's, and for a moment all was still along the wire. Then the voices burst forth again in a fury of excitement and fear.

"Git help!"

"We'll meet at Bishop's place."

And someone put in, "It's Abner Whateley done it!"

Sick with shock and half-paralyzed with a growing awareness, Abner struggled to tear the receiver from his ear, to shut off the half-crazed bedlam on the party line. He managed it with an effort. Confused, upset, frightened himself, he stood for a moment with his head leaning against the wall. His thoughts seethed around but one central point—the fact that the Dunwich rustics considered him somehow responsible for what was happening. And their conviction, he knew intuitively, was based on more than the countryman's conventional distrust of the stranger.

He did not want to think about what had happened to Luke Lang—and to those others. Luke's frightened agonized voice still rang in his ears. He pulled himself away from the wall, almost stumbling over one of the kitchen chairs. He stood for a moment beside the table, not knowing what to do, but as his mind cleared a little, he thought only of escape. Yet he was caught between the desire to get away and the obligation to Luther Whateley he had not yet fulfilled.

But he had come, he had gone through the old man's things—all save the books—he had made arrangements to tear down the mill part of the house—he could manage its sale through some agency; there was no need for him to be present. Impulsively, he hastened to the bedroom, threw such things as he had unpacked, together with Luther Whateley's note-filled ledger, into his bags and carried them out to his car.

Having done this, however, he had second thoughts. Why should he take flight? He had done nothing. No guilt of any kind rested upon him. He returned to the house. All was still, save for the unending chorus of frogs and whippoorwills. He stood briefly undecided; then he sat down at the table and took out Grandfather Whateley's final letter to read it once more.

He read it over carefully, thoughtfully. What had the old man meant when, in referring to the madness that had spawned among the Whateleys, he had said, "It has not been so of all that is mine," though he himself had kept free of that madness? Grandmother Whateley had died long before Abner's birth; his Aunt Julie had died as a young girl; his mother had led a blameless life. There remained Aunt Sarey. What had been her madness, then? Luther Whateley could have meant none other. Only Sarey remained. What had she done to bring about her imprisonment unto death?

And what had he intended to hint at when he adjured Abner to kill anything in the mill section of the house, anything that lived? *No matter how small it may be. No matter what form it may have* . . . Even something so small as an inoffensive toad? A spider? A fly? Luther Whateley wrote in riddles, which in itself was an affront to an intelligent man. Or did his grandfather think Abner a victim to the superstition of science? Ants, spiders, flies, various kinds of bugs, millers, centipedes, daddy longlegs—all occupied the old mill; and doubtless in its walls were mice as well. Did Luther Whateley expect his grandson to go about exterminating all these?

Behind him suddenly something struck the window. Glass fragmented to the floor, together with something heavy. Abner sprang to his feet and whirled around. From outside came the sound of running footsteps.

A rock lay on the floor amid the shattered glass. There was a piece of "store paper" tied to it by common store string. Abner picked it up, broke the string, and unfolded the paper.

Crude lettering stared up at him. "Git out before ye git kilt!" Store paper and string. It was not meant so much as a threat as a well-intentioned warning. And it was clearly the work of Tobias Whateley, thought Abner. He tossed it contemptuously to the table.

His thoughts were still in turmoil, but he had decided that precipitate flight was not necessary. He would stay, not only to learn if his suspicions about Luke Lang were true—as if the evidence of the telephone left room for doubt—but also to make a final attempt to fathom the riddle Luther Whateley had left behind.

He put out the light and went in darkness to the bedroom, where he stretched out, fully clothed, upon the bed.

Sleep, however, would not come. He lay probing the maze of his thoughts, trying to make sense out of the mass of data he had accumulated, seeking always that basic fact which was the key to all the others. He felt sure it existed; worse, he was positive that it lay before his eyes—he had but failed to interpret it or to recognize it.

He had been lying there scarcely half an hour, when he heard, rising above the pulsating choir of the frogs and whippoorwills, a splashing from the direction of the Miskatonic—an approaching sound, as if a large wave were washing up the banks on its seaward way. He sat up, listening. But even as he did so, the sound stopped and another took its place—one he was loath to identify, and yet could define as no other than that of someone trying to climb the mill wheel.

He slid off the bed and went out of the room.

From the direction of the shuttered room came a muffled, heavy falling sound—then a curious, choking whimpering that sounded horribly like a child at a great distance trying to call out—then all was still, and it seemed that even the noise and clamor of the frogs diminished and fell away.

He returned to the kitchen and lit the lamp.

Pooled in the yellow glow of light, Abner made his way slowly up the stairs toward the shuttered room. He walked softly, careful to make no sound.

Arriving at the door, he listened. At first he heard nothing—then a susurration smote his ears.

Something in that room—*breathed*!

Fighting back his fear, Abner put the key in the lock and turned it. He flung the door open and held the lamp high.

Shock and horror paralyzed him.

There, squatting in the midst of the tumbled bedding from

that long-abandoned bed, sat a monstrous, leathery-skinned creature that was neither frog nor man, one gorged with food, with blood still slavering from its batrachian jaws and upon its webbed fingers—a monstrous entity that had strong, powerfully long arms, grown from its bestial body like those of a frog, and tapering off into a man's hands, save for the webbing between the fingers. . . .

The tableau held for only a moment.

Then, with a frenzied growling sound—*Eh-ya-ya-ya-ya-haah-ngh'aaa-h'yuh, h'yuh*—it rose up, towering, and launched itself at Abner.

His reaction was instantaneous, born of terrible, shattering knowledge. He flung the kerosene-filled lamp with all his might straight at the thing reaching toward him.

Fire enveloped the thing. It halted and began to tear frantically at its burning body, unmindful of the flames rising from the bedding behind it and the floor of the room, and at the same instant the caliber of its voice changed from a deep growling to a shrill, high wailing—"*Mama-mama—ma-aa-ma-aa-ma-aaah*!"

Abner pulled the door shut and fled.

Down the stairs, half falling, through the rooms below, with his heart pounding madly, and out of the house. He tumbled into the car, almost bereft of his senses, half-blinded by the perspiration of his fear, turned the key in the ignition, and roared away from that accursed place from which the smoke already poured, while spreading flames in that tinder-dry building began to cast a red glow into the sky.

He drove like one possessed—through Dunwich—through the covered bridge—his eyes half-closed, as if to shut out forever the sight of that which he had seen, while the dark, brooding hills seemed to reach for him and the chanting whippoorwills and frogs mocked him.

But nothing could erase that final, cataclysmic knowledge seared into his mind—the key to which he had had all along and not known it—the knowledge implicit in his own memories as well as in the notes Luther Whateley had left—the chunks of raw meat he had childishly supposed were going to be prepared in Aunt Sarey's room instead of to be *eaten raw,* the reference to "R." who had come "back at last" after having escaped, back to the only home "R." knew—the seemingly unrelated references also in his grandfather's hand to missing cows, sheep, and the remains of other animals—the hideous suggestion clearly defined now in those entries of Luther Whateley's about R.'s "size commensurate with amt. of food," and "he must be kept on a careful diet and to a controllable size"—like the Innsmouth people!—controlled to nothingness after Sarah's death, with Luther hoping that foodless confinement might shrivel the thing in the shuttered room and kill it beyond revival, despite the doubt that had led him to adjure Abner to kill "anything in it that lives"—*the thing Abner had unwittingly liberated when he broke the pane and kicked out the shutters—liberated to seek its own food and its hellish growth again, at first with fish from the Miskatonic, then with small animals, then cattle, and at last human beings—the thing that was half-batrachian, half-human, but human enough to come back to the only home it had ever known and to cry out in terror for its mother in the face of the fatal holocaust—the thing that had been born to the unblessed union of Sarah Whateley and Ralsa Marsh, spawn of tainted and degenerate blood, the monster that would loom forever on the perimeter of Abner Whateley's awareness—his cousin Ralsa, doomed by his grandfather's iron will, instead of being released long ago into the sea to join the Deep Ones among the minions of Dagon and great Cthulhu!*

DARK DREAM

Elizabeth Fancett

THIS IS THE hour that I used to love, soft in the early morning, the sun fresh risen in the east, when the sands are gentle warm and the day is cool and even the sea is comparatively calm and peaceful—and safe.

Soon the sun will be hot and high, the beach a burning bed on which a thousand bodies laze and lie before they run to shed the scorch of day within the welcome coolness of the shining, rolling, thundering sea.

Today will be a good surfing day; like many others we have known, and he has loved, since we made this golden land our land, our home. How readily, and with what skill and ease, he took to this tremendous ocean, challenging it, mastering it, making it his own.

Sometimes it frightens me, how much he loves the sea. I do not share his love, and I swim no more powerfully than a child, and while he rides the rearing, rolling waters, I remain at the ocean's edge, among the laughing, playing children, content to watch and laugh with them, as they run from the mighty breakers roaring in to twist and lift their small brown bodies and toss them up like leaves onto the cool and golden sands. But, without him, I would not go even to the water's edge. And always there is a fear in me, a secret dread of this enormous ocean, so seeming blue in sunlight, so dark, so deep out there beyond these gentle shores.

And fear seeps into sleep and dreams are fashioned, turning those fears into thoughts and the thoughts into images, and the night takes up the living dreads of day; takes, draws out, re-forms into some monstrous pattern that the waking mind could never dare to contemplate.

The night before he went away, I had such a dream. I was here on this beach, waiting for his return, but it was later in the day than now and the sun was hot and high. I stood at the ocean's edge among the laughing, playing children. But I did not play and I did not laugh. I watched him as he waited, sixty or seventy yards out, among the other surfers to catch the next great breaker. I knew that he would take it easily, skillfully, in perfect balance, riding splendidly the fierce and foaming giant. I watched with love and pride—pride in his strength, his skill, his graceful tallness. And I watched with fear.

I saw the waves come sweeping in, swelling and rising, an enormous white-tipped wall of water as it came racing, rolling across the great ocean. As the giant breakers reared behind him the man next to him was spun into his path. I saw them both go down, the waves closing over. Presently, they surfaced apart, struck out to retrieve their skis.

He was swimming strongly, his powerful form cutting through the buffeting waters, was almost to his ski and reaching out for it, when suddenly he was flung, high and violently, out of the sea. For one brief moment I saw the sunlight glinting on his brown body as he hurtled into the air, and then he fell back and I could not see him and I knew that where he fell the sea was no longer blue—but red.

And there was a shout about me and cries of "Shark! Shark!" and a bell was ringing way back upon the beach and there were cries and screams of panic and of warning and the people in the sea were swimming desperately away from the danger, away from the widening, blood-red patch of foam . . . away from him . . . away from him . . . and the children screamed and scrambled from the sea and soon there were no people in the water or at its edge, save me.

I could not hear his screams of pain but I knew that he must be screaming, writhing in an agony of terror, in a grotesquely fearsome oneness with that great dark shape beneath the waters, its teeth locked tight about his brown limb, spinning him around like a mad dog with a bone, trying to wrench the limb away.

And then there were lifeguards running, and one already in the belt, and others coming. . . . But I was no longer on the shore. I was racing into the surf, tearing through the first great breaker, my one thought to reach him, to be with him—to die with him.

I surfaced, choking, beyond the breaker, swimming strongly, swimming desperately through the deep, tempestuous ocean that I so feared and hated, until my arms, my legs were aching, straining, weakening. But I would not let my body weaken, nor the buffeting, bruising, contemptuous sea hold me back from my beloved.

I was near now, close to the blood-red patch of foam. I trod water, easing my aching limbs, calling his name, willing him to rise above the ever-reddening foam. I called his name, I shrieked it. I could not hear my voice above the surf's roar. I could not see him, but he was there, struggling beneath the madly swirling waters as the thing beneath threshed and twisted and spun him savagely around, trying to tear his limb away.

A huge wave came rolling in, lifted me, smothered me, almost drowned me. I fought to surface, clawing upward, my eyes, my mouth full of sea. I rose, choking, blinded, my lungs bursting, my ears deafened with the roar of the endless thundering sea.

And suddenly there he was, his dear face white, agonized, and the water about him red with his blood. The water was full of blood.

I was close, so close. His hands reached out to me. I caught them, held them briefly before I felt a tremendous tug upon my straining arms, and I knew then that the shark had torn his limb away. His eyes closed in agony beyond describing and I could not hold him and his hands slid away from mine and he sank once more beneath the richly reddening foam. And the water was full of blood.

Then there was movement about me, and a face close to mine and other hands reaching out to me and I was screaming out his name and I tried to dive beneath that blood-red sea to find him, hold him, die with him. But I was caught and held in strong, relentless hands, and suddenly I saw his face again—a gray blob upon the surface of the sea, his eyes closed tight in agony or shock, or death, I knew not which. And then the great high sun was a glaring fire above me and the sea a roar and a rage about my face and body as I was pulled in a breathless rush of speed through the stinging, blinding, smothering waters. And somewhere I could hear a cry, and voices shouting, warning, and I knew that the shark was following in the trail of bloodied waters . . . in the trail of him. . . .

And then I was lying on the sands and my mind was screaming that this could not—must not—be, and that the morning soon would come and wake me from this dark and fearsome dream. And in my dream I was filled with dread that the morning would not come before I was forced to see its final horror. And the dream went on and I saw his brown and bloodied body lying there on the swiftly reddening sands, the blood still pouring from the raw and hideous wound where the shark had ripped his leg away, and they did not have to tell me that my beloved was dead.

And then it was morning and the sun was high, and he had left me to catch his early plane. He had gone quietly, without waking me, for he knows that I hate partings, however brief. I awoke to another week away from him.

But this is his job, that is our life; one that he had always wanted in this new enormous land of sun and sands and blue-white surfing waters.

Today, he is returning. That is why I wait here on this beach in this bright and savage, sunny place, where dark shapes lurk in darker waters beneath the blue-white breakers of the mighty sea. This is where he will find me—today when he returns. This has always been our custom and—despite my fears—our joy. And we would run and laugh together across the burning sands, we would run toward the waiting sea, and soon he would be where the giant breakers rise and rear beneath the surge and swell of it, the rising roar and roll of it, challenging, taking, riding it, and I would not have him be afraid—as I was afraid—of this blue and endless sea.

But now? Will I tell him of my dream, that by its telling it shall not come to pass? Can one prevent that which *will* happen? That is against all reason! Yet I must try—yes, I must try—although I know no power on earth or in heaven can alter what will be.

But *will* it be? Maybe it was only a *warning* dream. And yet—how can I tell him? *Will* I tell him? Will he not laugh, teasingly, and say: "All surfers know there may be sharks around. That's all part of the fun—the danger!" And he will say, trying to calm my fears: "At least, that's what we kid ourselves! But we all know that the real man-eaters—the blue pointers—haven't been seen around these coasts for years." And he will say, seeing that I am still afraid: "Forget it, darling! Dreams are just things that pass away with night and never, never come true!"

Already the sun is a glare on high, swift and fierce in its rising, the fire and bright and burn of it a haze of whiteness above the golden sands. The sea that merely moved and murmured in the cool calmness of the morning now rolls and stirs and summons up its awful power in the dark and dreadful deeps beyond the waiting, empty shore.

There is something wrong about the day! A few people scattered here and there about the sands, a child or two playing in small, safe pools along the shore. But there is no one in the sea. No one swims, no small brown bodies dare the tumbling rollers sweeping in toward the shoreline.

Out at sea a helicopter hovers, circles, flies on. There is a hush of waiting, a sense of danger . . . fear. . . .

I notice now that the warning flags are crossed against each other. Though I do not know the reason for them, I am grateful for the flags. At least today there will be no surfing. He will be disappointed—but he will not surf today.

There is a large notice farther down the beach—too far away for me to read. I see some lifeguards sitting, talking outside the club rooms. There is movement, a face, in the Shark Tower. I stroll toward the notice, read the bold words largely printed:

KILLER SHARK OFF THE COASTLINE.
ALL SWIMMING, SURFING PROHIBITED UNTIL
FURTHER NOTICE.

Killer shark! Two words of terror, warning, telling the world, telling him, in the full, clear light of the unsleeping, dreamless day.

There should be fear, horror in my eyes. Instead, they shine with joy. There should be ice in my heart. Instead, it is warm, light, it leaps, surges, sings. For it was, after all, a *warning* dream. No need now to tell him, no need now to try in desperate fear to make him heed the warning. For now that we *know,* it can be prevented. It need not happen. This is real, this notice, real these words, this sign that he can read, this order that he must obey.

A tall, bronzed man comes striding down the beach. My heart leaps, my feet tiptoe to run to meet him. But I see now it is just another lifeguard, making for the group by the clubhouse. I do not know him. I think he must be new at this beach. As he draws near, he glances curiously at me. I know that I am smiling, but I cannot help it.

"Do you think you'll catch him?" I ask, pointing to the warning notice.

His face is grim. "We're gunning for him," he says. "Not only here, but all along this coastline."

I stare at him. I had not thought of that. Why had I supposed it would be here, on *this* beach?

The lifeguard is saying: "No one's going to like the ban, of course—and I don't doubt some of them will try elsewhere—but at least there'll be no more surfing or swimming from *this* beach until the brute is caught!"

My heart is cold. What if *he* were to try another beach, to beat the ban, as many surfers would do?

My heart is ice. It still could happen as in my dream!

It still could be!

I walk with him toward the other lifeguards. I know them all, vaguely, by sight.

But there is one. . . . My heart thumps, painfully. *His* was the face close to mine, his the arms that held me, stayed me, kept me from dying with my love! This was the man who had held me close as I waited, screaming, for my dream to end. Yes, *this* was the beach, this the place of which I had been warned.

I am calm now, my heart eased with the knowledge that this brings. It would not be elsewhere, but here—if it were to happen. And it will not happen. It will not be. And I must not dwell upon the dream again. It is done with, forget it!

I try to break my thoughts, to listen to what the lifeguard is saying as we draw near to the group by the clubhouse. But memory of the dream persists, and I see again the swirling waters where the dark shape threshed and spun him around, tugging, wrenching, tearing, beneath the ever-reddening foam. I hear again the surf's relentless roar, feel that dreadful tug upon my arms, see his face, white with agony, his eyes full of pain and horror, his blood on the waters, his blood on the sand. . . .

"I hate the sea!"

My sudden cry startles my companion. Then he shrugs. "These things don't often happen," he says. "But when they do—I think we all hate the sea."

"I would never come," I say, "except to be with my husband. He comes here regularly—every day, in fact. He loves the sea."

He turns, looks at me. "You were here, maybe?" he asks. "Saw it happen? I'm sorry if you did. It must have been a grim experience."

"What?" I ask. "See what happen?"

"I was just telling you—the brute's already made a killing."

"Oh, no!" My voice is harsh, shocked, my heart tight with horror that already someone has known the reality of terror I have only known in dream.

"I haven't been here for a while," I tell him shakily. "My husband has been away."

"It happened last week," he is saying, "not sixty yards out. A blue pointer it was—an enormous brute. It had a girth of—" He broke off apologetically. "I'm sorry, you won't want to hear about it."

But again, I am not really listening. My gaze is fixed on the familiar face of the lifeguard in the group by the clubhouse. He turns, looks at me as we draw near. He is speaking now, softly, quietly, to one of his companions, who also turns, looks at me. He leaves the group, approaches me.

"You shouldn't be here," he is saying. His voice is gruff, his face grave, concerned.

"It's all right," I answer. "I'm waiting for my husband. He's been away, you see. I know that he can't surf today—and I'm glad—glad of the shark—in a way, that is. I don't want anyone to be hurt, and I'm sorry about the accident, but I'm glad he won't be allowed to surf, because he wouldn't pay heed to silly dreams, and last week I had this dream just before he went away. . . ." And then I am telling him of my dream, eagerly, in a rush and spill of anguished words, glad to speak of it, wanting to speak of it, knowing the need. And his eyes are full of pity as he listens and his face is dark and grave as through my words I live again that fearsome dream of his dark and dreadful death and spare myself no smallest detail in the grim remembering, until I am screaming that this could not, must not, be and the white-hot sands bite deep into my body as I fling myself still screaming to the burning ground, crying out for the morning soon to come and put an end to dreaming.

And then he is lifting me, soothing me, cradling me close, tight, and I look up into the familiar face of the man who holds me—as he held me then on that hot and savage, sunny day—and I know that the morning will not come and the dream will never, never end.

TWO SPINSTERS

E. Phillips Oppenheim

ERNESTON GRANT WAS without doubt a very first-class detective, but as a wayfarer across Devonshire byroads, with only a map and a compass to help him, he was simply a washout. Even his fat little white dog, Flip, sheltered under a couple of rugs, after two hours of cold, wet, and purposeless journeying, looked at him reproachfully. With an exclamation of something like despair, Grant brought his sobbing automobile to a standstill at the top of one of the wickedest hills a Ford had ever been asked to face and sat looking around him.

In every direction the outlook was the same. There were rolling stretches of common divided by wooded valleys of incredible depth. There was no sign of agricultural land, no sign of the working of any human being upon the endless acres, and not a single vehicle had Grant passed upon the way. There were no sign-posts, no villages, no shelter of any sort. The one thing that abounded was rain—rain and mist. Gray wreaths of it hung over the commons, making them seem like falling fragments of cloud, blotted out the horizon, hung over every hopeful break in the distance—an encircling, enveloping obscurity.

Then, vying with the mists in wetness, came the level

rain—rain which had seemed beautiful early in the afternoon, slanting from the heavens onto the mountainside, but which had long ago lost all pretense to being anything but damnably offensive, chilling, miserably wet. Flip, whose nose only now appeared uncovered, sniffed disgustedly, and Grant, as he lit a pipe, cursed slowly but fluently under his breath. What a country! Miles of byways without a single direction post, endless stretches without a glimpse of a farmhouse or village. And the map! Grant solemnly cursed the man who had ordained it, the printer who had packaged it, and the shop where he had bought it. When he had finished, Flip ventured upon a gentle bark of approval.

"Somewhere or other," Grant muttered to himself, "should lie the village of Nidd. The last sign-post in this blasted region indicated six miles to Nidd. Since then we have traveled at least twelve, there has been no turning to the left or to the right, and the village of Nidd is as though it had never been."

His eyes pierced the gathering darkness ahead. Through a slight uplifting in the clouds it seemed to him that he could see for miles, and nowhere was there any sign of village or of human habitation. He thought of the road along which they had come, and the idea of retracing it made him shiver. It was at that moment, when bending forward to watch the steam from his boiling radiator, that he saw away on the left a feebly flickering light. Instantly he was out of the car. He scrambled onto the stone wall and looked eagerly in the direction from which he had seen it.

There was without doubt a light; around that light must be a house. His eyes could even trace the rough track that led to it. He climbed back to his place, thrust in his clutch, drove for about forty yards, and then paused at a gate. The track on the other side was terrible, but then so was the road. He opened it and drove through, bending over his task now with every sense absorbed.

Apparently traffic here, if traffic existed at all, consisted only of an occasional farm wagon of the kind he was beginning to know all about—springless, with holes in the boarded floor and with great, slowly turning wheels. Nevertheless he made progress, passed, to his joy, a semi-cultivated field, through another gate, up, it seemed, suddenly into the clouds, and down a fantastic corkscrew way, until at last the light faced him directly ahead. He passed a deserted garden and pulled up before a broken-down iron gate, which he had to get out of the car to open. He punctiliously closed it after him, traversed a few yards of grass-grown, soggy ground, and finally reached the door of what might once have been a very tolerable farmhouse, but which appeared now, notwithstanding the flickering light burning upstairs, to be one of the most melancholy edifices the mind of man could conceive.

With scant anticipation in the way of a welcome, but with immense relief at the thought of a roof, Grant descended and knocked upon the oak door. Inside be could hear almost at once the sound of a match being struck; the light of a candle shone through the blindless windows of a room on his left. There were footsteps in the hall, and the door was opened. Grant found himself confronted by a woman who held the candle so high that it half illumined, half shadowed her features. There was a certain stateliness, however, about her figure, which he realized even in those first few seconds at the door.

"What do you want?" she asked.

Grant, as he removed his hat, fancied that the answer was sufficiently obvious. Rain streamed from every angle of his be-mackintoshed body. His face was pinched with the cold.

"I am a traveler who has lost his way," he explained. "For hours I have been trying to find a village and inn. Yours is the first human habitation I have seen. Can you give me a night's shelter?"

"Is there anyone with you?" the woman inquired.

"I am alone," he replied. "Except for my little dog," he added, as he heard Flip's hopeful yap.

The woman considered.

"You had better drive your car into the shed on the left-hand side of the house," she said. "Afterward, come in. We will do what we can for you. It is not much."

"I am very grateful, madam," Grant declared in all sincerity.

He found the shed, which was occupied only by two farm carts in an incredible state of decay. Afterward he released Flip and returned to the front door, which had been left open. Guided by the sound of crackling logs, he found his way to a huge stone kitchen. In a high-backed chair in front of the fire, seated with her hands upon her knees but gazing eagerly toward the door as though watching for his coming, was another woman, also tall, approaching middle age, perhaps, but still of striking presence and fine features. The woman who had admitted him was bending over the fire. He looked from one to the other in amazement. They were fearfully and wonderfully alike.

"It is very kind of you, ladies, to give us shelter," he began. "Flip! Behave yourself, Flip!"

A huge sheep dog had occupied the space in front of the fire. Flip, without a moment's hesitation, had run toward him, yapping fiercely. The dog, with an air of mild surprise, rose to his feet and looked inquiringly downward. Flip insinuated herself into the vacant place, stretched herself out with an air of content, and closed her eyes.

"I must apologize for my little dog," Grant continued. "She is very cold."

The sheep dog retreated a few yards and sat on his haunches, considering the matter. Meanwhile the woman who had opened the door produced a cup and saucer from a cupboard, a loaf of bread, and a small side of bacon, from which she cut some slices.

"Draw your chair to the fire," she invited. "We have very little to offer you, but I will prepare something to eat."

"You are good Samaritans indeed," Grant declared fervently.

He seated himself opposite the woman who as yet had scarcely spoken or removed her eyes from his. The likeness between the two was an amazing thing, as was also their silence. They wore similar clothes—heavy, voluminous clothes they seemed to him—and their hair, brown and slightly besprinkled with gray, was arranged in precisely the same fashion. Their clothes belonged to another world, as did also their speech and manners, yet there was a curious but unmistakable distinction about them both.

"As a matter of curiosity," Grant asked, "how far am I from the village of Nidd?"

"Not far," the woman who was sitting motionless opposite to him answered. "To anyone knowing the way, near enough. Strangers are foolish to trust themselves to these roads. Many people are lost who try."

"Yours is a lonely homestead," he remarked.

"We were born here," the woman answered. "Neither my sister nor I have felt the desire for travel."

The bacon began to sizzle. Flip opened one eye, licked her mouth, and sat up. In a few minutes the meal was ready. A high-backed oak chair was placed at the end of the table. There was tea, a platter of bacon and eggs, a great loaf of bread, and a small pat of butter. Grant took his place.

"You have had your supper?" he asked.

"Long ago," the woman who had prepared his meal replied. "Please to serve yourself."

She sank into the other oak chair exactly opposite her sister. Grant, with Flip by his side, commenced his meal. Neither had tasted food for many hours, and for a time both were happily oblivious to anything except the immediate surroundings.

Presently, however, as he poured out his second cup of tea, Grant glanced toward his hostesses. They had moved their chairs slightly away from the fire and were both watching him—watching him without curiosity, yet with a certain puzzling intentness. It occurred to him then for the first time that, although both had in turn addressed him, neither had addressed the other.

"I can't tell you how good this tastes," Grant said presently. "I am afraid I must seem awfully greedy."

"You have been for some time without food, perhaps," one of them said.

"Since half past twelve."

"Are you traveling for pleasure?"

"I thought so before today," he answered, with a smile to which there was no response.

The woman who had admitted him moved her chair an inch or two nearer to his. He noticed with some curiosity that immediately she had done so her sister did the same thing.

"What is your name?"

"Erneston Grant," he replied. "May I know whom I have to thank for this hospitality?"

"My name is Mathilda Craske," the first one announced.

"And mine is Annabelle Craske," the other echoed.

"You live here alone?" he asked.

"We live here entirely alone," Mathilda answered. "It is our pleasure."

Grant was more than ever puzzled. Their speech was subject to the usual Devonshire intonation and soft slurring of the vowels, but otherwise it was almost curiously correct. The idea of their living alone in such a desolate place, however, seemed incredible.

"You farm here, perhaps?" he persisted. "You have laborers' cottages, or someone close at hand?"

Mathilda shook her head.

"The nearest hovel," she confided, "is three miles distant. We have ceased to occupy ourselves with the land. We have five cows—they give us no trouble—and some fowls."

"It is a lonely life," he murmured.

"We do not find it so," Annabelle said stiffly.

He turned his chair toward them. Flip, with a little gurgle of satisfaction, sprang onto his knees.

"Where do you do your marketing?" he asked.

"A carrier from Exford," Mathilda told him, "calls every Saturday. Our wants are simple."

The large room, singularly empty of furniture, as he noticed, looking around, was full of shadowy places, lit only by the single oil lamp. The two women themselves were only dimly visible. Yet every now and then in the flickering firelight he caught a clearer glimpse of them. They were so uncannily alike that they might well be twins. He found himself speculating as to their history. They must once have been very beautiful.

"I wonder whether it will be possible," he asked, after a somewhat prolonged pause, "to encroach further upon your hospitality and beg for a sofa or a bed for the night? . . . Anyplace will do," he added hastily.

Mathilda rose at once to her feet. She took another candle from the mantelpiece and lit it.

"I will show you," she said, "where you may sleep."

For a moment Grant was startled. He had happened to glance toward Annabelle and was amazed at a sudden curious expression —an expression almost of malice in her face. He stooped to bring her into the little halo of lamplight more completely and stared at her incredulously. The expression, if ever it had been there, had vanished. She was simply looking at him patiently with something in her face which he failed utterly to understand.

"If you will follow me," Mathilda invited.

Grant rose to his feet. Flip turned around with a final challenging bark to the huge sheep dog, who had accepted a position remote from the fire, and, failing to elicit any satisfactory response, trotted after her master. They passed into a well-shaped but almost empty hall, up a broad flight of oak stairs to the first landing. Outside the room from which Grant had seen the candlelight, she paused for a moment and listened.

"You have another guest?" he inquired.

"Annabelle has a guest," she replied. "You are mine. Follow me, please."

She led the way to a bedchamber in which was a huge four-poster and little else. She set the candle upon a table and turned down a sort of crazy quilt that covered the bedclothes. She felt the sheets and nodded approvingly. Grant found himself unconsciously following her example. To his surprise they were warm. She pointed to a great brass bed warmer with a long handle at the farther end of the room, from which a little smoke was still curling upward.

"You were expecting someone tonight?" he asked curiously.

"We are always prepared," she answered.

She left the room, apparently forgetting to wish him good night. He called out pleasantly after her, but she descended the stairs. Then again there was silence—silence down below, silence in the part of the house where he was. Flip, who was sniffing around the room, at times showed signs of excitement, at times growled. Grant, opening the window, discovered a cigaret.

"Don't know that I blame you, old girl," he said. "It's a queer place."

Outside there was nothing to be seen and little to be heard save the roaring of a water torrent close at hand and the patter of rain. He suddenly remembered his bag and, leaving the door of his room open, descended the stairs. In the great stone kitchen the two women were seated exactly as they had been during his first meal with them. They both looked at him but neither spoke.

"If you don't mind," he explained, "I want to fetch my bag from the car."

Mathilda, the woman who had admitted him, nodded acquiescence. He passed out into the darkness, stumbled his way to the shed, and unstrapped his bag. Just as he was turning away he thrust his hand into the tool chest and drew out a flashlight, which he slipped into his pocket. When he reentered the house the two women were still seated in their chairs and still silent.

"A terrible night," he remarked. "I can't tell you how thankful I am to you for so hospitably giving me shelter."

They both looked at him but neither made any reply. This time when he reached his room he closed the door firmly, and noticed with a frown of disappointment that except for the latch there was no means of fastening it. Then he laughed to himself softly. He, the famous captor of Ned Bullivant, the victor in a score of scraps with desperate men, was suddenly nervous in this lonely farmhouse inhabited by a couple of strange women.

"Time I took a holiday," he muttered to himself. "We don't understand nerves, do we, Flip?" he added.

Flip opened one eye and growled. Grant was puzzled.

"Something around here she doesn't like," he ruminated. "I wonder who's in the room with the lighted candles?"

He opened his own door once more, softly, and listened. The silence was almost unbroken. From downstairs in the great kitchen he could hear the ticking of a clock, and he could see the thin streak of yellow light underneath the door. He crossed the landing and listened for a moment outside the room with the candles. The silence within was absolute and complete—not even the sound of the ordinary breathing of a sleeping person. He retraced his steps, closed his own door, and began to undress. At the bottom of his bag was a small automatic pistol. His fingers played with it for a moment. Then he threw it back. His flashlight, however, he placed by the side of his bed. Before he turned in, he leaned once more out of the window. The roar of the falling water seemed more insistent than ever. Otherwise there was no sound. The rain had ceased, but the sky was black and starless. With a little shiver he turned away and climbed into bed.

He had no idea of the time but the blackness outside was just as intense when he was suddenly awakened by Flip's low growling. She had shaken herself free from the coverlet at the foot of the bed and he could see her eyes, wicked little spots of light, gleaming through the darkness. He lay quite still for a moment, listening. From the first he knew that there was someone in the room. His own quick intuition had told him that, although he was still unable to detect a sound. Slowly his hand traveled out to the side of the bed. He took up his flashlight and turned it on. Then, with an involuntary cry, he shrank back. Standing within a few feet of him was Mathilda, still fully dressed, and in her hand, stretched out toward him, was the cruelest-looking knife he had ever seen. He slipped out of bed, and honestly and self-confessedly afraid, kept the light fixed upon her.

"What do you want?" he demanded, amazed at the unsteadiness of his own voice. "What on earth are you doing with that knife?"

"I want *you,* William," she answered, a note of disappointment in her tone. "Why do you keep so far away?"

He lit the candle. The finger which on the trigger of his automatic had kept Bullivant with his hands up for a life-long two minutes, was trembling. With the light in the room now established, however, he felt more himself.

"Throw that knife on the bed," he ordered, "and tell me what you were going to do with it."

She obeyed at once and leaned a little toward him.

"I was going to kill you, William," she confessed.

"And why?" he demanded.

She shook her head sorrowfully.

"Because it is the only way," she replied.

"My name isn't William, for one thing," he objected, "and what do you mean by saying it is the only way?"

She smiled, sadly and disbelievingly.

"You should not deny your name," she said. "You are William Foulsham. I knew you at once, though you had been away so long. When *he* came," she added, pointing toward the other room, "Annabelle believed that *he* was William. I let her keep him. I knew. I knew if I waited, you would come."

"Waiving the question of my identity," he struggled on, "why do you want to kill me? What do you mean by saying it is the only way?"

"It is the only way to keep a man," she answered. "Annabelle and I found that out when you left us. You knew each of us loved you, William; you promised each of us never to leave—do you remember? So we sat here and waited for you to come back. . . . We said nothing, but we both knew."

"You mean that you were going to kill me to keep me here?" he persisted.

She looked toward the knife lovingly.

"That isn't killing," she said. "Don't you see—you could never go away. You would be here with us always."

He began to understand, and a horrible idea stole into his brain.

"What about the man she thought was William?" he asked.

"You shall see him if you like," she answered eagerly. "You shall see how peaceful and happy he is. Perhaps you will be sorry then that you woke up. Come with me."

He possessed himself of the knife and followed her out of the room and across the landing. Underneath the door he could see the little chink of light—the light that had been his beacon from the road. She opened the door softly and held the candle over her head. Stretched upon another huge four-poster bed was the figure of a man with a ragged, untidy beard. His face was as pale as the sheet, and Grant knew from the first glance that he was dead. By his side, seated stiffly in a high-backed chair, was Annabelle. She raised her finger and frowned as they entered. She looked across at Grant.

"Step quietly," she whispered. "William is asleep."

Just as the first gleam of dawn was forcing a finger of light through the sullen bank of clouds, a distraught and disheveled-looking man, followed by a small fat white dog, stumbled into the village of Nidd, gasped with relief at the sight of the brass plate upon a door, and pulled the bell for all he was worth. Presently a window was opened and a man's shaggy head thrust out.

"Steady there!" he expostulated. "What's the trouble with you, anyway?"

"I've spent a part of the night in a farmhouse a few miles from here," he shouted. "There's a dead man there and two madwomen, and my car's broken down."

"A dead man?" the doctor repeated.

"I've seen him. My car's broken down in the road, or I should have been here before."

"I'll be with you in five minutes," the doctor promised.

Presently the two men were seated in the doctor's car on their way back to the farm. It was light now, with signs of clearing, and in a short time they drew up in front of the farmhouse. There was no answer to their knock. The doctor turned the handle of the door and opened it. They entered the kitchen. The fire was out, but, each in her high-backed chair, Mathilda and Annabelle were seated, facing one another, speechless, yet with wide-open eyes. They both turned their heads as the two men entered. Annabelle nodded with satisfaction.

"It is the doctor," she said. "Doctor, I am glad that you have come. You know, of course, that William is back. He came for me. He is lying upstairs, but I cannot wake him. I sit with him and hold his hand and I speak to him, but he says nothing. He sleeps so soundly. Will you wake him for me, please? I will show you where he lies."

She led the way from the room, and the doctor followed her. Mathilda listened to their footsteps. Then she turned to Grant with that strange smile once more upon her lips.

"Annabelle and I do not speak," she explained. "We quarreled just after you went away. We have not spoken for so many years that I forget how long it is. I should like someone to tell her, though, that the man who lies upstairs is *not* William. I should like someone to make her realize that *you* are William, and that you have come back for *me*. Sit down, William. Presently, when the doctor has gone, I will build the fire and make you some tea."

Grant sat down and again he felt his trembling. The woman looked at him kindly.

"You have been gone a long time," she continued. "I should have known you anywhere, though. It is strange that Annabelle does not recognize you. Sometimes I think we have lived together so long here that she may have lost her memory. I am glad you fetched the doctor, William. Now Annabelle will know her mistake."

There was the sound of footsteps descending the stairs. The doctor entered. He took Grant by the arm and led him to one side.

"You were quite right," he said gravely. "The man upstairs is a poor traveling tinker who has been missing for over a week. I should think that he has been dead at least four days. One of us must stay here while the other goes to the police station."

Grant caught feverishly at his hat.

"*I* will go for the police," he said.

THE WAY UP TO HEAVEN

Roald Dahl

ALL HER LIFE, Mrs. Foster had had an almost pathological fear of missing a train, a plane, a boat, or even a theater curtain. In other respects, she was not a particularly nervous woman, but the mere thought of being late on occasions like these would throw her into such a state of nerves that she would begin to twitch. It was nothing much—just a tiny vellicating muscle in the corner of the left eye, like a secret wink—but the annoying thing was that it refused to disappear until an hour or so after the train or plane or whatever it was had been safely caught.

It is really extraordinary how in certain people a simple apprehension about a thing like catching a train can grow into a serious obsession. At least half an hour before it was time to leave the house for the station, Mrs. Foster would step out of the elevator all ready to go, with hat and coat and gloves, and then, being quite unable to sit down, she would flutter and fidget about from room to room until her husband, who must have been well aware of her state, finally emerged from his privacy and suggested in a cool, dry voice that perhaps they had better get going now, had they not?

Mr. Foster may possibly have had a right to be irritated by this foolishness of his wife, but he could have had no excuse for increasing her misery by keeping her waiting unnecessarily. Mind you, it is by no means certain that this is what he did, yet whenever they were to go somewhere, his timing was so accurate—just a minute or two late, you understand—and his manner so bland that it was hard to believe he wasn't purposely inflicting a nasty private little torture of his own on the unhappy lady. And one thing he must have known—that she would never dare to call out and tell him to hurry. He had disciplined her too well for that. He must also have known that if he was prepared to wait even beyond the last moment of safety, he could drive her nearly into hysterics. On one or two special occasions in the later years of their married life, it seemed almost as though he had *wanted* to miss the train simply in order to intensify the poor woman's suffering.

Assuming (though one cannot be sure) that the husband was guilty, what made his attitude doubly unreasonable was the fact that, with the exception of this one small irrepressible foible, Mrs. Foster was and always had been a good and loving wife. For over thirty years, she had served him loyally and well. There was no doubt about this. Even she, a very modest woman, was aware of it, and although she had for years refused to let herself believe that Mr. Foster would ever consciously torment her, there had been times recently when she had caught herself beginning to wonder.

Mr. Eugene Foster, who was nearly seventy years old, lived with his wife in a large six-story house in New York City, on East Sixty-Second Street, and they had four servants. It was a gloomy place, and few people came to visit them. But on this particular morning in January, the house had come alive and there was a great deal of bustling about. One maid was distributing bundles of dust sheets to every room, while another was draping them over the furniture. The butler was bringing down suitcases and putting them in the hall. The cook kept popping up from the kitchen to have a word with the butler, and Mrs. Foster herself, in an old-fashioned fur coat and with a black hat on the top of her head, was flying from room to room and pretending to supervise these operations. Actually, she was thinking of nothing at all except that she was going to miss her plane if her husband didn't come out of his study soon and get ready.

"What time is it, Walker?" she said to the butler as she passed him.

"It's ten minutes past nine, madam."

"And has the car come?"

"Yes, madam, it's waiting. I'm just going to put the luggage in now."

"It takes an hour to get to Idlewild," she said. "My plane leaves at eleven. I have to be there half an hour beforehand for the formalities. I shall be late. I just *know* I'm going to be late."

"I think you have plenty of time, madam," the butler said kindly. "I warned Mr. Foster that you must leave at nine fifteen. There's still another five minutes."

"Yes, Walker, I know, I know. But get the luggage in quickly, will you, please?"

She began walking up and down the hall, and whenever the butler came by, she asked him the time. This, she kept telling herself, was the one plane she must not miss. It had taken months to persuade her husband to allow her to go. If she missed it, he might decide that she should cancel the whole thing. And the trouble was that he insisted on coming to the airport to see her off.

"Dear God," she said aloud, "I'm going to miss it, I know, I know, I *know* I'm going to miss it." The little muscle beside the left eye was twitching madly now. The eyes themselves were very close to tears.

"What time is it, Walker?"

"It's eighteen minutes past, madam."

"Now I really *will* miss it!" she cried. "Oh, I wish he would come!"

This was an important journey for Mrs. Foster. She was going all alone to Paris to visit her daughter, her only child, who was married to a Frenchman. Mrs. Foster didn't care much for the Frenchman, but she was fond of her daughter, and more than that, she had developed a great yearning to set eyes on her three grandchildren. She knew them only from the many photographs that she had received and that she kept putting up all over the house. They were beautiful, these children. She doted on them, and each time a new picture arrived she would carry it away and sit with it for a long time, staring at it lovingly and searching the small faces for signs of that old satisfying blood likeness that meant so much. And now, lately, she had come more and more to feel that she did not really wish to live out her days in a place where she could not be near these children, and have them visit her, and take them for walks, and buy them presents, and watch them grow. She knew, of course, that it was wrong and in a way disloyal to have thoughts like these while her husband was still alive. She knew also that, although he was no longer active in his many enterprises, he would never consent to leave New York and live in Paris. It was a miracle that he had ever agreed to let her fly over there alone for six weeks to visit them. But, oh, how she wished she could live there always, and be close to them!

"Walker, what time is it?"

"Twenty-two past, madam."

As he spoke, a door opened and Mr. Foster came into the hall. He stood for a moment, looking intently at his wife, and she looked back at him—at this diminutive but still quite dapper old man with the huge bearded face that bore such an astonishing resemblance to those old photographs of Andrew Carnegie.

"Well," he said, "I suppose perhaps we'd better get going fairly soon if you want to catch that plane."

"Yes, dear—*yes*! Everything's ready. The car's waiting."

"That's good," he said. With his head over to one side, he was watching her closely. He had a peculiar way of cocking the head and then moving it in a series of small, rapid jerks. Because of this and because he was clasping his hands up high in front of him, near the chest, he was somehow like a squirrel standing there—a quick, clever old squirrel from the park.

"Here's Walker with your coat, dear. Put it on."

"I'll be with you in a moment," he said. "I'm just going to wash my hands."

She waited for him, and the tall butler stood beside her, holding the coat and the hat.

"Walker, will I miss it?"

"No, madam," the butler said. "I think you'll make it all right."

Then Mr. Foster appeared again, and the butler helped him on with his coat. Mrs. Foster hurried outside and got into the hired Cadillac. Her husband came after her, but he walked down the steps of the house slowly, pausing halfway to observe the sky and to sniff the cold morning air.

"It looks a bit foggy," he said as he sat down beside her in the car. "And it's always worse out there at the airport. I shouldn't be surprised if the flight's canceled already."

"Don't say that, dear—*please.*"

They didn't speak again until the car had crossed over the river to Long Island.

"I arranged everything with the servants," Mr. Foster said. "They're all going off today. I gave them half-pay for six weeks and told Walker I'd send him a telegram when we wanted them back."

"Yes," she said. "He told me."

"I'll move into the club tonight. It'll be a nice change, staying at the club."

"Yes, dear. I'll write to you."

"I'll call in at the house occasionally to see that everything's all right and to pick up the mail."

"But don't you really think Walker should stay there all the time to look after things?" she asked meekly.

"Nonsense. It's quite unnecessary. And anyway, I'd have to pay him full wages."

"Oh, yes," she said. "Of course."

"What's more, you never know what people get up to when

they're left alone in a house," Mr. Foster announced, and with that he took out a cigar and, after snipping off the end with a silver cutter, lit it with a gold lighter.

She sat still in the car with her hands clasped together tight under the rug.

"Will you write to me?" she asked.

"I'll see," he said. "But I doubt it. You know I don't hold with letter writing unless there's something specific to say."

"Yes, dear, I know. So don't you bother."

They drove on, along Queen's Boulevard, and as they approached the flat marshland on which Idlewild is built, the fog began to thicken and the car had to slow down.

"Oh, dear!" cried Mrs. Foster. "I'm *sure* I'm going to miss it now! What time is it?"

"Stop fussing," the old man said. "It doesn't matter anyway. It's bound to be canceled now. They never fly in this sort of weather. I don't know why you bothered to come out."

She couldn't be sure, but it seemed to her that there was suddenly a new note in his voice, and she turned to look at him. It was difficult to observe any change in his expression under all that hair. The mouth was what counted. She wished, as she had so often before, that she could see the mouth clearly. The eyes never showed anything except when he was in a rage.

"Of course," he went on, "if by any chance it *does* go, then I agree with you—you'll be certain to miss it now. Why don't you resign yourself to that?"

She turned away and peered through the window at the fog. It seemed to be getting thicker as they went along, and now she could only just make out the edge of the road and the margin of grassland beyond it. She knew that her husband was still looking at her. She glanced at him again, and this time she noticed with a kind of horror that he was staring intently at the little place in the corner of her left eye where she could feel the muscle twitching.

"Won't you?" he said.

"Won't I what?"

"Be sure to miss it now if it goes. We can't drive fast in this muck."

He didn't speak to her any more after that. The car crawled on and on. The driver had a yellow lamp directed onto the edge of the road, and this helped him to keep going. Other lights, some white and some yellow, kept coming out of the fog toward them, and there was an especially bright one that followed close behind them all the time.

Suddenly, the driver stopped the car.

"There!" Mr. Foster cried. "We're stuck. I knew it."

"No, sir," the driver said, turning around. "We made it. This is the airport."

Without a word, Mrs. Foster jumped out and hurried through the main entrance into the building. There was a mass of people inside, mostly disconsolate passengers standing around the ticket counters. She pushed her way through and spoke to the clerk.

"Yes," he said. "Your flight is temporarily postponed. But please don't go away. We're expecting the weather to clear any moment."

She went back to her husband, who was still sitting in the car, and told him the news. "But don't you wait, dear," she said. "There's no sense in that."

"I won't," he answered. "So long as the driver can get me back. Can you get me back, driver?"

"I think so," the man said.

"Is the baggage out?"

"Yes, sir."

"Good-bye, dear," Mrs. Foster said, leaning into the car and giving her husband a small kiss on the coarse gray fur of his cheek.

"Good-bye," he answered. "Have a good trip."

The car drove off, and Mrs. Foster was left alone.

The rest of the day was a sort of nightmare for her. She sat for hour after hour on a bench, as close to the airline counter as possible, and every thirty minutes or so she would get up and ask the clerk if the situation had changed. She always received the same reply—that she must continue to wait, because the fog might blow away at any moment. It wasn't until after six in the evening that the loudspeakers finally announced that the flight had been postponed until eleven o'clock the next morning.

Mrs. Foster didn't quite know what to do when she heard this news. She could stay sitting on the bench the whole night through. That would be the safest. But she was already exhausted, and it didn't take her long to realize that this was a ridiculous thing for an elderly lady to do. So in the end she went to a phone and called the house.

Her husband, who was on the point of leaving for the club, answered it himself. She told him the news, and asked whether the servants were still there.

"They've all gone," he said.

"In that case, dear, I'll just get myself a room somewhere for the night. And don't you bother yourself about it at all."

"That would be foolish," he said. "You've got a large house here at your disposal. Use it."

"But, dear, it's *empty*."

"Then I'll stay with you myself."

"There's no food in the house. There's nothing."

"Then eat before you come in. Don't be so stupid, woman. Everything you do, you seem to want to make a fuss about it."

"Yes," she said. "I'm sorry. I'll get myself a sandwich here, and then I'll come on in."

Outside, the fog had cleared a little, but it was still a long, slow drive in the taxi, and she didn't arrive back at the house on Sixty-Second Street until fairly late.

Her husband emerged from his study when he heard her coming in. "Well," he said, standing by the study door, "how was Paris?"

"We leave at eleven in the morning," she answered. "It's definite."

"You mean if the fog clears."

"It's clearing now. There's a wind coming up."

"You look tired," he said. "You must have had an anxious day."

"It wasn't very comfortable. I think I'll go straight to bed."

"I've ordered a car for the morning," he said. "Nine o'clock."

"Oh, thank you, dear. And I certainly hope you're not going to bother to come all the way out again to see me off."

"No," he said slowly. "I don't think I will. But there's no reason why you shouldn't drop me at the club on your way."

She looked at him, and at that moment he seemed to be standing a long way off from her, beyond some borderline. He was suddenly so small and far away that she couldn't be sure what he was doing, or what he was thinking, or even what he was.

"The club is downtown," she said. "It isn't on the way to the airport."

"But you'll have plenty of time, my dear. Don't you want to drop me at the club?"

"Oh, yes—of course."

"That's good. Then I'll see you in the morning at nine."

She went up to her bedroom on the second floor, and she was so exhausted from her day that she fell asleep soon after she lay down.

Next morning, Mrs. Foster was up early, and by eight thirty she was downstairs and ready to leave.

Shortly after nine, her husband appeared. "Did you make any coffee?" he asked.

"No, dear. I thought you'd get a nice breakfast at the club. The car is here. It's been waiting. I'm all ready to go."

They were standing in the hall—they always seemed to be meeting in the hall nowadays—she with her hat and coat and purse, he in a curiously-cut Edwardian jacket with high lapels.

"Your luggage?"

"It's at the airport."

"Ah, yes," he said. "Of course. And if you're going to take me to the club first, I suppose we'd better get going fairly soon, hadn't we?"

"Yes!" she cried. "Oh, yes—*please*!"

"I'm just going to get a few cigars. I'll be right with you. You get in the car."

She turned and went out to where the chauffeur was standing, and he opened the car door for her as she approached.

"What time is it?" she asked him.

"About nine fifteen."

Mr. Foster came out five minutes later, and watching him as he walked slowly down the steps, she noticed that his legs were like goat's legs in those narrow stovepipe trousers that he wore. As on the day before, he paused halfway down to sniff the air and to examine the sky. The weather was still not quite clear, but there was a wisp of sun coming through the mist.

"Perhaps you'll be lucky this time," he said as he settled himself beside her in the car.

"Hurry, please," she said to the chauffeur. "Don't bother about the rug. I'll arrange the rug. Please get going. I'm late."

The man went back to his seat behind the wheel and started the engine.

"*Just* a moment!" Mr. Foster said suddenly. "Hold it a moment, chauffeur, will you?"

"What is it, dear?" She saw him searching the pockets of his overcoat.

"I had a little present I wanted you to take to Ellen," he said. "Now, where on earth is it? I'm sure I had it in my hand as I came down."

"I never saw you carrying anything. What sort of present?"

"A little box wrapped up in white paper. I forgot to give it to you yesterday. I don't want to forget it today."

"A little box!" Mrs. Foster cried. "I never saw any little box!" She began hunting frantically in the back of the car.

Her husband continued searching through the pockets of his coat. Then he unbuttoned the coat and felt around in his jacket. "Confound it," he said, "I must've left it in my bedroom. I won't be a moment."

"Oh, *please*!" she cried. "We haven't got time! *Please* leave it!

You can mail it. It's only one of those silly combs anyway. You're always giving her combs."

"And what's wrong with combs, may I ask?" he said, furious that she should have forgotten herself for once.

"Nothing, dear, I'm sure. But . . ."

"Stay here," he commanded. "I'm going to get it."

"Be quick, dear! Oh, *please* be quick!"

She sat still, waiting and waiting.

"Chauffeur, what time is it?"

The man had a wristwatch, which he consulted. "I make it nearly nine thirty."

"Can we get to the airport in an hour?"

"Just about."

At this point, Mrs. Foster suddenly spotted a corner of something white wedged down in the crack of the seat on the side where her husband had been sitting. She reached over and pulled out a small paper-wrapped box, and at the same time she couldn't help noticing that it was wedged down firm and deep, as though with the help of a pushing hand.

"Here it is!" she cried. "I've found it! Oh, dear, and now he'll be up there forever searching for it! Chauffeur, quickly—run in and call him down, will you, please?"

The chauffeur, a man with a small rebellious Irish mouth, didn't care very much for any of this, but he climbed out of the car and went up the steps to the front door of the house. Then he turned and came back. "Door's locked," he announced. "You got a key?"

"Yes—wait a minute." She began hunting madly in her purse. The little face was screwed up tight with anxiety, the lips pushed outward like a spout.

"Here it is! No—I'll go myself. It'll be quicker. I know where he'll be."

She hurried out of the car and up the steps to the front door, holding the key in one hand. She slid the key into the keyhole and was about to turn it—and then she stopped. Her head came up, and she stood there absolutely motionless, her whole body arrested right in the middle of all this hurry to turn the key and get into the house, and she waited—five, six, seven, eight, nine, ten seconds, she waited. The way she was standing there, with her head in the air and the body so tense, it seemed as though she were listening for the repetition of some sound that she had heard a moment before from a place far away inside the house.

Yes—quite obviously she was listening. Her whole attitude was a *listening* one. She appeared actually to be moving one of her ears closer and closer to the door. Now it was right up against the door, and for still another few seconds, she remained in that position, head up, ear to door, hand on key, about to enter but not entering, trying instead, or so it seemed, to hear and to analyze these sounds that were coming faintly from this place deep within the house.

Then, all at once, she sprang to life again. She withdrew the key from the door and came running back down the steps.

"It's too late!" she cried to the chauffeur. "I can't wait for him. I simply can't. I'll miss the plane. Hurry now, driver, hurry! To the airport!"

The chauffeur, had he been watching her closely, might have noticed that her face had turned absolutely white and that the whole expression had suddenly altered. There was no longer that rather soft and silly look. A peculiar hardness had settled itself upon the features. The little mouth, usually so flabby, was now tight and thin, the eyes were bright, and the voice, when she spoke, carried a new note of authority.

"Hurry, driver, hurry!"

"Isn't your husband traveling with you!" the man asked, astonished.

"Certainly not! I was only going to drop him at the club. It won't matter. He'll understand. He'll get a cab. Don't sit there talking, man. *Get going!* I've got a plane to catch for Paris!"

With Mrs. Foster urging him from the back seat, the man drove fast all the way, and she caught her plane with a few minutes to spare. Soon she was high up over the Atlantic, reclining comfortably in her airplane chair, listening to the hum of the motors, heading for Paris at last. The new mood was still with her. She felt remarkably strong and, in a queer sort of way, wonderful. She was a trifle breathless with it all, but this was more from pure astonishment at what she had done than anything else, and as the plane flew farther and farther away from New York and East Sixty-Second Street, a great sense of calmness began to settle upon her. By the time she reached Paris, she was just as strong and cool and calm as she could wish.

She met her grandchildren, and they were even more beautiful in the flesh than in their photographs. They were like angels, she told herself, so beautiful they were. And every day she took them for walks, and fed them cakes, and bought them presents, and told them charming stories.

Once a week, on Tuesdays, she wrote a letter to her husband—a nice, chatty letter—full of news and gossip, which always ended with the words, "Now be sure to take your meals regularly, dear, although this is something I'm afraid you may not be doing when I'm not with you."

When the six weeks were up, everybody was sad that she had to return to America, to her husband. Everybody, that is, except her. Surprisingly, she didn't seem to mind as much as one might have expected, and when she kissed them all good-bye, there was something in her manner and in the things she said that appeared to hint at the possibility of a return in the not too distant future.

However, like the faithful wife she was, she did not overstay her time. Exactly six weeks after she had arrived, she sent a cable to her husband and caught the plane back to New York.

Arriving at Idlewild, Mrs. Foster was interested to observe that there was no car to meet her. It is possible that she might even have been a little amused. But she was extremely calm and did not overtip the porter who helped her into a taxi with her baggage.

New York was colder than Paris, and there were lumps of dirty snow lying in the gutters of the streets. The taxi drew up before the house on Sixty-Second Street, and Mrs. Foster persuaded the driver to carry her two large cases to the top of the steps. Then she paid him off and rang the bell. She waited, but there was no answer. Just to make sure, she rang again, and she could hear it tinkling shrilly far away in the pantry, at the back of the house. But still no one came.

So she took out her own key and opened the door herself.

The first thing she saw as she entered was a great pile of mail lying on the floor where it had fallen after being slipped through the letter box. The place was dark and cold. A dust sheet was still draped over the grandfather clock. In spite of the cold, the atmosphere was peculiarly oppressive, and there was a faint and curious odor in the air that she had never smelled before.

She walked quickly across the hall and disappeared for a moment around the corner to the left, at the back. There was something deliberate and purposeful about this action; she had the air of a woman who is off to investigate a rumor or to confirm a suspicion. And when she returned a few seconds later, there was a little glimmer of satisfaction on her face.

She paused in the center of the hall, as though wondering what to do next. Then, suddenly, she turned and went across into her husband's study. On the desk she found his address book, and after hunting through it for a while she picked up the phone and dialed a number.

"Hello," she said. "Listen—this is Nine East Sixty-Second Street. . . . Yes, that's right. Could you send someone around as soon as possible, do you think? Yes, it seems to be stuck between the second and third floors. At least, that's where the indicator's pointing . . . Right away? Oh, that's very kind of you. You see, my legs aren't any too good for walking up a lot of stairs. Thank you so much. Good-bye."

She replaced the receiver and sat there at her husband's desk, patiently waiting for the man who would be coming soon to repair the lift.